Calliope

By Jan Dearman

For information, or to order additional copies,
please contact:

Beacon Publishing Group
P.O. Box 41573 Charleston, S.C. 29423
800.817.8480| beaconpublishinggroup.com

Publisher's catalog available by request.

ISBN-13: 978-1-949472-59-2

ISBN-10: 1-949472-59-2

Published in 2023. New York, NY 10001.

First Edition. Printed in the USA.

Calliope

Dedicated to all the Calliopes,

who add richness and interest to life with their
unique natures and gifts ...

and to those of us who love them.

Chapter 1

"Mom, we're going to have to stop. I'm getting sick."

"Jess, I told you to get your head out of that game," Johnna McGregor reprimanded her daughter. "I warned you before we started up the mountain, it's just one curve after another, and you have to focus on the road."

Jess huffed, "Yes, just curves and trees and rocks for miles and miles!"

"And beauty if you'd just let yourself appreciate it. Occasionally you can see the creek down there," Johnna tilted her head toward the driver's side window. "It's really rolling after all the rain they've had."

Jess did not respond, leaning back on the head rest and taking deep breaths. Next to her, Charlie, rubbing his eyes, awakened from his nap in the car seat and asked, "Mommy, are we most all there yet?"

Johnna smiled at the sweetness of his almost three-year old voice. Glimpsing his still sleepy face in the rearview mirror, she replied, "Yes, Precious, just about five more miles."

Turning to Jess, Charlie held up his open hand and said, "This many, Sissy."

For a moment Jess forgot her nausea, as she smiled and responded, "Yes, Sweet Charlie," and kissed his pudgy hand. She loved him so much. The eight years between them brought no feeling of jealousy or rivalry—an occasional bit of annoyance when he interrupted her privacy, but mostly she felt an overwhelming desire to

1

cuddle and protect this small masculine image of herself. She was glad she shared with Charlie the brunette hair and heavily lashed silver-gray eyes that were their father's unusual traits. Charlie would know him only as a handsome pilot in a photograph—Lieutenant Colonel J. B. McGregor in his flight suit, helmet under his arm, standing next to the Fighting Falcon. But Jess would make sure he would be in Charlie's mind the same heroic figure he remained in her memory.

Charlie was barely a year old when their father's test plane went down in the Mojave. Jess thought their life had been perfect. A happy family, they shared so much fun and laughter. Her beautiful mother and handsome father were loving and affectionate with each other—Dad called her mother "Gorgeous" and said her hair gleamed like gold in the desert sun. Theirs was her ideal of the romance and marriage she wanted when she grew up. But now, he was gone, the fairy tale had ended, and there could not be another man like her father. His disappearance had brought a cloud of sadness and a feeling of withdrawal from the joy and hope of the future she once visualized for herself.

Tears threatened as Jess again cast her eyes down to the game in her hands. So, what if she felt sick? She always felt sick, but she seldom threw up. Now, they were moving away from California, away from home, away from the place her father loved, back to her mother's birthplace in the Appalachians. She felt like only half a person—the sad, ugly, hopeless half. She could only see dark, threatening clouds. The happy half with its blue sky and sun was lost when her father disappeared in a thunderous, fiery burst in the very midst of a warm, fair summer day.

Chapter 2

Johnna had exhausted all her resources, for Jess and herself. She had followed her husband wherever his assignments had taken him, even to the last, which took him to his death. She knew J. B. was a heroic figure in the eyes of her sensitive, intelligent daughter. Never would Jess know or understand the challenges and anxieties of living with a man who found his joy and excitement in a career that routinely was a gamble for his survival and the unity and stability of his family. Johnna had to fight her own feeling of guilt over not being as supportive, perhaps, as other pilots' wives. She tried to be positive and not to show worry when she knew he would be testing. She was not a creature who loved to soar above the earth—she wanted her feet on the ground, no matter how rocky the surface might be.

Johnna had sought the help of the base counselors, experts in dealing with grief and its impact on wives and children, but nothing seemed to crack or chip away the clouded bubble of despondency that engulfed her daughter. And nothing assuaged Johnna's feeling of swimming in a dark, endless sea with no rescue in sight.

Flying back home to Tennessee was a struggle she endured for the sake of travel time and the children's comfort. The six-hour trip was an exciting adventure for Charlie, when he wasn't sleeping soundly, and Jess' gaze rarely left the porthole. Johnna knew Jess was thinking of J. B., and she wondered if her daughter might feel nearer to him in the realm of his demise. Even with Charlie's energy and excitement, the three-hour layover in Salt Lake City was a welcome relief for Johnna. They snacked on over-priced treats and bought costly souvenirs for Grandma and themselves. But Johnna knew this was a once in her lifetime, one-way trip. She didn't bother to look at price tags.

She was coming home to mountains that wrapped their arms around her shoulders in familiar greeting; to the cold, roiling creeks gurgling into the Tennessee that flowed along the lowland's edge; to the home where her mother's calm and patient nature, hopefully, would be a salve for their troubled, hurting souls. She would begin a new chapter in her life and, prayerfully, in the lives of her children. She wanted Jess to be the happy, silly, carefree pre-teen she should be. She wanted Charlie to grow up in the solid security of not only a contented, stable family structure, but in an environment that would challenge his thinking and learning about the beauty of creation, not about the adventure and thrills he might find flying above it, as did J. B. She loved her husband with all the potential for love within her, but she didn't want her son to follow in J. B.'s "flight path." And she wanted Jess to realize her dad, though a great husband and father, chose to gamble and give his life for something he loved as much, if not more, she thought, than his own wife and children. His choice took his life from the family who loved him—from the wife whose heart ached for him, from the daughter who idolized him, and from the son who would never know him, leaving them broken and sadly in need of repair.

Chapter 3

At the foot of the mountain, their path took a sharp right at the river road cutoff and began the final two miles to their grandmother's house. Grandma Craig had flown to California for Dad's memorial service, but Jess had been distressed and confused. She had little remembrance of Grandma's visit.

Jess had been to the cottage on the mountain only once—a couple of years before Charlie was born. At the time, she thought of it as a magical place, a gabled house of mountain stone tucked into a matching retaining wall. White shuttered mullioned front windows boasted white flowerboxes filled with red geraniums. Steps brought one up to a concrete porch beneath the windows, where an array of pots held other plants and flowers, and a couple of bent willow rockers looked out over the rise to the river below. To the left of the porch, on the same level, a patch of grass surrounded a small dogwood tree growing up before the kitchen window, and a pebbled walkway led around the corner of the cottage to the kitchen door. To the right of the porch, more steps rose to an upper landing and the arched wooden front door. Jess remembered Grandma's house as being like a picture in the book of fairy tales she now read to Charlie. The recollection gave her no pleasure; there was no sentimentality in the memories, only facts and features.

"Jess, your grandmother is eager to see you and Charlie. Please be polite and friendly. She hasn't seen you in a long time, and she's spent very little time with Charlie. You need to help him feel comfortable until he gets used to Grandma and her house."

Jess didn't respond. She knew Grandma loved her and would want her to show affection. In her head, Jess knew she loved—she loved her mother, and she loved her grandmother, but there was no feeling, no wanting, no tears of anything but loss. Charlie was the only light in her dark tunnel of despair.

"Jess, did you hear me?" Her mother's voice sounded irritated and a bit frightened.

Jess knew she was being a drag on her mother, and she couldn't understand or control at times the compulsion to punish her mother with distant silence. What had her mother ever done to Jess or their family—except to live, to move forward, and to compel Jess to go with her? "Yes, ma'am, I heard you."

Charlie interrupted her thoughts: "Mommy, Sissy, look—a big boat!" He excitedly pointed toward the river and the long vessel forging its way upstream.

"Charlie, it's really just one small boat—a tugboat, and it's pushing barges that carry coal and lumber and other things, called cargo. It's a very strong little boat—a powerful pusher," she smiled.

"A tugboat," he repeated thoughtfully. "I want to be a tugboat." Jess repressed a smile.

"Well, you can't be a tugboat—you're a little boy. But you could grow up and be a tugboat pilot … a tugboat captain," Johnna corrected herself, with a twinge of regret the word pilot so easily entered her vocabulary.

Johnna pulled into the driveway and parked. "Jess, just leave the bags. We'll see your grandmother and unload the car later." Jess unbuckled Charlie as her mother came around to the back seat, extricated Charlie from his remaining restraints, and scooped him up in her arms. Jess exited her side of the car, grabbing her Nintendo before she slammed the door. They proceeded up the path to the porch, where Grandma Craig had awaited their arrival.

Her grandmother met them halfway. She was wearing jeans and a blue chambray work shirt, and her white hair was pulled back in a neat ponytail. Without a word, Grandma Craig enveloped her daughter and Charlie in a warm embrace. Jess saw tears coursing her mother's cheek, as Johnna said softly, "Oh, Mama, I'm so glad to be home. I've missed you."

Grandma Craig replied, "Yes, dear, I've missed you, too." Then she looked at her daughter, brushed a wisp of hair from Johnna's face, and caressed her cheek. Grandma took Charlie's hand and kissed it, as Charlie, unsure of his response to this new person, leaned his head against his mother.

Turning to Jess, Grandma said, "And Jess, how you have grown! And so beautiful!" Jess said, "Hi, Grandma" and moved toward Lily Craig to allow her a hug. She released Jess but held her shoulders and said to her: "Jess, you are the very image of your father. He was a such a good man. I couldn't have ordered a finer husband for my daughter. I loved him very much." She smiled and continued: "I think he thought me a pretty good mother-in-law, too, especially since I stayed on the other side of the country most of the time."

Jess saw her mother smile. But not knowing how to respond, she pulled away and waited for someone to make a move, to move her, to give her direction. She didn't know what they expected of her or if she could give it.

"Let's get you settled in your rooms. Then we can unload the car." Grandma turned and made her way to the

porch steps. "Johnna, I've got you and little man in the
guest room. Jess, I thought you might like to stay in your
mother's old room. There's no telling what interesting
stuff you may find in there—and you're free to roam,
pillage and plunder to your heart's content."

Jess followed them through the wooden front door
and into the vestibule. An antique mirrored hall tree on the
left supported a red denim barn jacket on one of its brass
hooks. On the right, next to the hallway to her
grandmother's private annex, a rustic mahogany console
table held a rectangular basket for mail and car keys, and
a thriving philodendron flowed to the slate floor.

The entry transitioned into rich oak flooring in the
living/dining room, through which they proceeded past the
bookcase-lined fireplace to the guest bedroom and half-
bath. "I've put a toddler bed in here for Charlie," Lily said,
"so he can be near, and you can have the bed to yourself,
unless you just want to snuggle," she smiled.

Jess was waiting outside the guest room, noting the
framed photos lining the fireplace mantle: her mother's
high school graduation picture … her parents cutting their
wedding cake, her father resplendent in his dress uniform
and her mother, slim and golden in a lace sheath, her hair
in an elegant chignon adorned with roses … a school
picture of Jess at age 8 … Charlie's baby picture … her
grandmother and the grandfather she never knew, seated
at a poolside table in a tropical locale … and a photo of the
young man Jess assumed was her mother's older brother,
Jeff, who died in a hunting accident before Jess was born.

"Now, Jess, let's get you situated," her
grandmother directed, as she crossed in front of the
bookcase to the opposite bedroom. "You can have the
bathroom next door for your own use, except when your
mother wants to bathe Charlie in the tub."

Lily opened the door to the former bedroom of her daughter, and memories of her earlier visit flooded Jess' mind. Light periwinkle blue enveloped the world of Johnna's youth—the walls, the bedspread, the velvet cover of the window seat ensconced in a nook of white mullioned windows looking out on azalea bushes, not yet in bloom. Beyond, Jess saw flowering dogwoods surrounding a huge rock projecting from the hill side. "I think you'll be comfortable here," Lily continued. "I've changed the mattresses in both rooms to memory foam, like I have in my bedroom in the add-on. Really comfy."

"Thanks, Grandma. I'm sure I'll be comfortable," Jess responded.

"The closet is mostly empty, except for clothing your mother left behind years ago. I've never removed them. You might even find something in there you'd like to try on, if only for fun and not for wearing. They're way out of style," she chuckled.

"Thanks, Grandma. I think I'll lie down if you don't mind. I was feeling a little carsick coming over the mountain. I'd like to rest a while."

"Surely, dear. We'll eat an early supper about five." Lily Craig moved to leave the room, then stopped to say, "Jess, I know you've had a terribly dark and distressing time since your dad's death. I hope you can find a bit of peace and healing while you are here. Your dad loved this place. He always said with that smile of his, 'If I had to be grounded, I'd be grounded here in these mountains.'" With quiet words, "I love you, Jess," she shut the door gently behind her, leaving her granddaughter with her thoughts.

Chapter 4

Johnna entered the kitchen to the evocative aroma of chicken and dumplings. "Oh, mom, my favorite. I haven't smelled that smell in years—and I know the taste will be even better."

"Well, dear, I want to bring back all the good memories I can." Lily added salt and pepper to the buttery chicken broth. "There's a fresh pot of coffee and gingersnaps in the cookie jar, if you want a little something before supper. Where's Charlie?"

"Oh, he's playing with his little people and barn animals on the living room floor. He's making himself right at home."

"Oh, I hope so." Her mother continued: "Johnna, do you remember the last time you and J. B. were here, and I fixed chicken and dumplings? I thought he would make himself sick, he ate so much. He said he'd be over flight weight when he got back to base."

Johnna paused, took a seat at the kitchen table, and replied, "Mom, I try not to think too much about J. B. It's too painful."

Lily covered the cooking pot and left the stew to simmer. She poured two cups of coffee and set them on the table. Then, she placed the cookie jar between them, commanding, "Johnna, eat a cookie—or, better, eat two or three."

"What? Eat a cookie?"

"Yes, eat a cookie. A cookie is one of the simplest

pleasures in this very short life. In fact, it may even be a metaphor for life itself—sweetness and satisfaction, if only a few bites, as long as it's your cookie of choice."

"Mom, you're not making any sense." Johnna frowned and shook her head.

"No, I guess I'm not." Lily pulled out a chair and sat, then sipped her coffee. "Johnna, I'm proud of you for the strength that's moving you to make a new life for you and the children. But you have to make a new 'normal' for the three of you, and that 'normal' needs to include J. B. Stop trying not to think about him. Accept the pain, feel the hurt, until it fades—and it will. But make J. B. a part of your life and the children's—allow the memories to be open and real, even if it means tears and angry outbursts from a grieving child."

"Oh, mom, I don't know if that's possible. Grief counselors haven't even helped. You just don't know how hard it's been."

"Johnna, you forget—I know it's hard—and I know it's possible. I was not much older than you when your dad died, and I nearly lost my mind with grief over your brother's accident."

Johnna's eyes misted and she whispered, "Mom, I'm sorry. I wasn't thinking."

Lily placed her hand over Johnna's and said, "Don't apologize, dear. I've lived through the worst days—the days like yours now. But your days are threatening to go on way too long. It's time you work on a new life with J. B.'s memories, not a life of constantly struggling to put him out of your mind, just so you won't feel pain. If you had not had a great love and a wonderful life with J. B., you wouldn't be hurting now. Be thankful for the blessing you've had."

"You're right, Mom. I know." Johnna, eyes closed,

rubbed her temples, as if to ease the building pressure of troublesome thoughts. "And I know I've got to help Jess—try to reestablish a good relationship with her. These years will be challenging enough, without the disruption of this move ... the burden of J. B.'s death ... the distance between us." Her voice trailed away, as she concluded: "So much to build and repair, I'm just not sure I know how to begin."

Lily held further comment, saying only, "Well, maybe being here will make a difference, and you both will find some answers." She returned to the kitchen counter and began making dough for the dumplings, as she added under her voice, "I know someone who just might be able to help." She smiled to herself when she heard the movement of the lid on the cookie jar.

Chapter 5

Listless, Jess had no desire to zone out with any of her games or to move her belongings into the room. Sitting on the side of the bed, she stared at the view through the wall of glass panes. She clicked the switch on the white hobnail lamp on the bedside table, then shut the blinds, sat on the window seat, and observed her surroundings. How long, she wondered, would this room be her enclosure? She didn't know her mother's plans for their new life in Tennessee—she wasn't sure even her mother knew. She hadn't asked and her mother hadn't told her. There were so many unanswered questions: Where would they live? Where would she go to school? Would her mother get a job and, if she did, who would care for Charlie? Would Jess ever see again the friends she had left in California, more than two thousand miles away?

With a sigh of resignation, Jess decided to make a preliminary inspection of the bedroom. It was simple, uncluttered, yet decidedly feminine—neat and attractive, like her mother. As she faced the bed from the window seat, she noted the mirrored French Provincial triple dresser to her left. On it rested a pink satin brocade jewelry box that Jess opened to reveal a divided compartment holding earrings, pins, and coins. Two shallow drawers beneath it held bracelets and necklaces. Jess didn't investigate further, but simply closed the lid and opened the dresser's drawers to see they were empty. Obviously, her grandmother had made room for Jess to unpack and store her clothes, indicating this would not be a short, "live out of the suitcase" visit.

On the other side of the bed was a desk that matched the dresser in style. A desk lamp like the one on the nightstand stood next to a writing set—desk pad, pen and pencil holder, and matching pastel floral portfolio holding a thick, fresh pad of lined paper. The single drawer held a book labeled "Journal" from the same set and pink file folders marked "Writing," "Tests," and "Grade Reports." With a grain of curiosity, Jess started to remove the diary, then closed the drawer on any impulse to inspect its secrets.

The wall to the right of the desk was a closet with white louvered folding doors. Jess pulled the doorknobs to expand the opening, revealing hanging clothes and jackets pushed to one side, sturdy white hangers ready for use, on the floor a large basket holding shoes and boots, and an assortment of decorative boxes on the overhead shelf. Again, Grandma Craig had made ample space for storage of Jess' things. Collecting her thoughts for a moment, Jess remembered the task ahead—retrieving luggage from the minivan they had rented in Nashville.

Jess entered the kitchen to find her mother, cookie in hand, sitting at the table with a cup of coffee and Grandma dropping slices of dough into the stewpot. "Hey there, dear," Grandma Craig addressed her. "Hope you're feeling better. If you like, have a cookie. There's milk in the fridge."

"Thanks, but I think I'll get my suitcase and backpack from the car. Is it locked, Mom?"

"Yes, the keys are on the table at the front door." Johnna addressed Lily: "A habit, locking up … security, vigilance, just part of daily life in California."

With an unseen sneer of displeasure at her mother's criticism of California, Jess left the kitchen to get the keys.

Chapter 6

"Lately security's a concern even around here," Lily informed her. "Well-to-do outsiders have discovered us. They're building fancy river homes down the road. They bring valuables with them that attract the less than reputable, who know the law is a long way away."

Johnna asked her mother, "Do you still feel safe here, Mom?"

"Oh, yes, dear. I don't mean to worry you. I'm part of the landscape around here—a mountain icon, you might say. My neighbors are far-flung, but they know Lily Craig is here to feed the hungry and help the needy as I can, so they keep an eye out for trouble. Remember the time Bonnie Gooden called to warn me about the 'stranger in black running up the road'?" She laughed. "It was just J. B. trying to work off some of the chicken and dumplings."

Johnna looked down at her cup and smiled. "I had forgotten about that."

"And they know I don't have anything worth stealing, except a bit of time and advice now and then." As an afterthought, Lily added: "Oh, and, of course, I have Fritz … and Luke Ferguson has made it his habit to check on me a couple of evenings a week." Chuckling, she added, "I know a hot supper has something to do with that."

"Oh, I hadn't even thought about Fritz. Where is he?" Johnna asked, reminded of the large Alsatian that was Lily's companion and protector, the most recent in a line of shepherds, Labs, and even a Doberman, who had received her expert training and loving care and had reciprocated with unfailing obedience and loyalty.

"He's in the mini-barn up the hill." Lily gestured toward the kitchen door. He has food and water up there, and he knows to stay until I call him. I thought he might frighten Charlie. I want to introduce them slowly, so Charlie will be comfortable around him. I know Fritz won't be a threat to Charlie, but Charlie might be too afraid to let him be the friend and protector I know Fritz can be."

Johnna was thoughtful as her mother moved about the kitchen. Lily released the steam on the pressure cooker to finish the fresh green beans. She sliced a loaf of friendship bread and took a congealed salad from the refrigerator. She was returning from the pantry with a booster seat, when Johnna asked, "Mom ... Luke Ferguson ... why is that name so familiar?"

Lily pulled a chair from the table and attached the seat for Charlie. Then, she sat down, looked at Johnna, and replied, "He was with your brother when Jeff shot himself. Luke applied the tourniquet to Jeff's leg and, on his back, carried Jeff out of the woods to the truck. Luke got Jeff to the hospital." Lily paused. "But Jeff had just lost too much blood."

Johnna frowned. Her mind was whirling, and tears threatened. "But ... how can you ... how can Luke Ferguson be so welcome in your life? How can you not feel the grief, the pain, every time you see his face, knowing he was part of what happened to Jeff?"

"Because he was part of what happened to Jeff. He was Jeff's best friend, he loved Jeff, and he tried his best to save him. When I arrived at the hospital, I first saw Luke in the waiting room, sobbing, covered in Jeff's blood. When the doctor came to tell us Jeff was gone, we were there for each other. We've been close ever since that day. Luke, grief … death … they've formed a bond that is special … strong … even comforting in a way." Lily stood and moved toward the dish cabinet. "How about you go get the children cleaned up for supper, while I finish?"

Johnna moved robotically through the tasks as directed—gather Charlie, put away his toys, tell Jess to get ready for supper, wash Charlie's face and hands, straighten her own hair and freshen her face. All the while, she tried to settle and understand the confusion of thoughts bumping around in her head.

Chapter 7

Jess tossed her backpack on the bed and rolled her suitcase to the open closet. Her three spring outfits, packed last, were first out of the bag: a simple gray dress and matching jacket with white buttons, a blue sundress and white sweater embroidered with blue flowers, and a navy jumper and long-sleeved blouse with navy polka dots. Jess was taller and appeared older than her eleven years, and she was glad she didn't have to wear frilly "little girl" stuff. She preferred a tee shirt and jeans—or khakis for school, but her mother said she would need dresses for Sunday services with Grandma. Her nicest dress she had left in California. At the memorial, her friend Gina had admired the black and white sundress, so Jess gave it to her—she never wanted to see it again. She wished she could discard as easily the terrible image of the explosion that nightly disturbed her sleep.

Jess put her khaki pants on hangers, then rolled the bag to the dresser to put away shirts and jeans. There was a knock on the door. "Yes?" she replied.

"It's Mom. Grandma said to clean up for dinner. May I come in?"

Jess, kneeling next to her suitcase in front of the lowest drawers, paused. "Okay."

Johnna entered the room and surveyed the familiar surroundings. "I loved this room." Jess heard sadness in her mother's voice. "Anything you find in here that you like is yours for the keeping. The rest I'll go through and either store it or trash it." Her mother moved to the dresser and opened the jewelry box to peruse its contents. "I had forgotten this." She picked up a charm bracelet chunky with silver memories. "Every one of these marks an event or something special to me at the time. I put the last charm on when I left for college—this orange and white UT pennant." Johnna shook the bracelet making it jingle, then dropped it back in the box and closed the lid. "Well, Charlie's already in his booster, so come soon or he'll get fussy."

"Yes, ma'am," Jess responded, as Johnna left the room, closing the door behind her. Jess opened the jewelry box, took out the bracelet, and held it in her hands to feel its weight. Surely it would have been too heavy and noisy for her mother to wear all those years ago when she was a teenager. Dropping it back in the drawer, Jess thought she'd look through the charms later and see what else might hide in the box.

Jess finished drying her hands on the back of her jeans as she entered the kitchen. The delicious smells of chicken and warm bread made her realize just how hungry she was. They had finished their airport snacks on the way to Grandma's, but that was hours ago. Jess took a seat at the table as Lily place bowls heaping with chicken and dumplings on each mat and accompanying plates with green beans and fruit salad. In the center she set a platter of sliced and buttered homemade bread.

"It's simple fare," Grandma declared, "but I think it'll taste pretty good after your travels today." Charlie picked up a green bean, but Lily held his arm and said, "Let's say the blessing first, Charlie. Let's thank God for our food. Do you want to say it since you're the little man with us today?"

Charlie put the bean back on his plate, folded his chubby baby hands, and said, "Thank you God for the food … for Mommy … for Jess … for Grandma … and Charlie! Amen." He picked up the bean and popped it in his mouth before he could be stopped again.

Jess could not remember when food had tasted so good. She showed her appreciation by consuming a second bowl of the stew and more cold milk. "This is really good, Grandma," she commented. "Thank you."

"Oh, yes, Mom," Johnna agreed. "Even better than I remembered it."

Lily said, "I'm glad you enjoyed it, but there's more if you're not too full. Jess, your mother's favorite dessert when she was your age was yellow cake with milk chocolate frosting—oh, and a scoop of vanilla ice cream."

Surprised, Jess looked at her mother, who, she knew, was careful about diet and exercise. Johnna declared, "Mom, you haven't? I'm going to gain five pounds this one meal!"

"Well, I have, and you could stand to put on five pounds!" Lily went to the pantry to retrieve an old-fashioned aluminum-domed cake plate she set on the counter. "Jess, if you'll get the tub of vanilla from the freezer, I'll cut the cake and you can scoop the ice cream into the bowls—in the dish drainer," she said, pointing with the cake knife.

They concentrated on their dessert in silence, interrupted occasionally by Charlie's "Umm, good!" Johnna leaned over and put her hand on Charlie's stomach. She said, "Charlie Boy, your tummy is so tight, I think you might pop." Charlie giggled and patted the taut red stripes of his tee shirt. "Pop! Charlie go pop!" Jess laughed and Charlie repeated, "Charlie go pop!" He was full of more giggles and increasing exuberance, as they laughed as he shouted, "Charlie go POP!"

Chapter 8

It had been a long time since Johnna had shared with her children such a moment, simply the result of chicken, dumplings, and layer cake. She was thankful and prayed there would be more such times. She sensed a glimmer of hope in Jess' open response to the sweet innocence of Charlie's joy and laughter.

"Johnna, why don't you get the children's sweaters, and we'll go out on the porch while it's still daylight. I'll put the food away and set the dishes in the sink. Then, we'll introduce Jess and Charlie to my friend Fritz."

"Fwitz?" Charlie asked. "I see Fwitz?"

"Mom, I'll get our sweaters, if you want to help Grandma," Jess suggested. Johnna noted the unsolicited offer from her daughter—a rare thing in the months of distance between them.

Lily responded, "Why, thanks, Jess. Your mom and I will get the kitchen cleaned up and join you and Charlie on the porch when we're finished."

Having left the rockers for Johnna and their grandmother, Jess and Charlie were sitting on the porch step, playing with Charlie's finger puppets. There was a slight chill in the early evening breeze. Though reminded of California's warmth, Johnna relished the feeling of freshness in the spring evening.

"Charlie, will you come sit with Grandma?" Lily

asked her grandson. Charlie shook his finger puppets into Jess' lap and said, "Uh-huh." He moved to the rocker, and Lily picked him up and settled him on her knees facing her. She said, "I told you I want you to meet my friend, Fritz."

"Fwitz," repeated Charlie, nodding his head in agreement.

"Well," Lily continued, "Fritz is a big dog. He is my friend and stays with me all the time. I want you to like him. I know he will like you. I don't want you to be afraid of him—he is very big. But he's like a friendly giant who will love you and protect you."

"Fwitz my friend, too," Charlie stated.

Lily said, "Yes, I want him to be your friend—and Jess' friend."

"My friend." Charlie declared, looking at his sister, who covered her smile with her hand.

Lily repeated, "Your friend and Jess' friend, okay?" Charlie pursed his brow but said, "Okay." Lily reached into the pocket of her barn jacket, brought out a whistle, and blew several quick blows, the signal for Fritz to come. In seconds, the massive Alsatian was sitting by Lily's side, and Charlie was glued to his grandmother's chest, his eyes wide with surprise and fear. The wolf-like dog was nearly as tall as Charlie and three times his weight. "Jess, come here and let Fritz get to know you. Then, maybe, Charlie will be comfortable."

Jess moved gingerly toward Fritz, trusting her grandmother's guidance. Lily said, "Fritz. Friend. Easy. Jess, let him smell your hand. Now, pat his head with your other hand." Lily pulled a treat from her pocket. "Now, give him this." Jess held the treat toward the dog, as Lily said, "Easy, Fritz." Fritz delicately took the dog biscuit from Jess' fingers. "Charlie, you want to give Fritz a cookie?" Charlie, now curious, sat up and took the treat Lily offered. "Hold it like this between your fingers and say, 'Easy, Fritz.'" Charlie did as directed, saying, "Easy, Fwitz." Again, the dog gently took the morsel from the little fingers. Charlie laughed, turned to Lily, and exclaimed, "Fwitz my friend!"

Johnna watched her children as they opened themselves to this new experience. Her mother had a reputation for dog handling and training, but she was amazed at the control Lily had over the creature—and the obvious allegiance of the dog for his mistress. This loyalty Lily now directed the dog to share with her grandchildren. She said, "Fritz, down," and the dog lay at her feet. Lily set Charlie down next to Fritz and said, "Now, Charlie, pet him if you want to."

Charlie stated, "Fwitz, you my friend" and rubbed the dog's head and back. Fritz, contented with the attention, licked the little boy's face, and Charlie cried with glee, "He kissed me!" Again, Johnna was thankful to share the simple joy of the moment.

Johnna joined her children and the dog in friendly companionship until the sky began to gray. Lily said, "Charlie, girls, it's been a long day for all of us. Let's go in and get some rest. We'll rise early in the morning, I'll fix us a good breakfast, and then we'll see what kind of excitement we can stir up."

Jess was sitting next to Fritz's warm body, and Charlie was lying with his head on the dog's broad back. He said, "No, I stay with Fritz."

Lily said, "Charlie, you are tired and need to rest so we can have fun tomorrow. Fritz will be with us inside while we sleep. He will keep us all safe."

"Okay," Charlie agreed and kissed Fritz's head. Johnna picked up the sleepy child, who said, "Night-night,

Fwitz."

Johnna said, "Tell Grandma goodnight and blow her a kiss."

"Night-night, Grandma. Come, Jess," he motioned to his sister.

Grandma Craig said, "Fritz wants to tell you goodnight." She signaled the dog to sit, then, to bark twice.

Lily said, "Good boy," and Johnna and Jess laughed as Charlie clapped his hands and said, "He can talk!"

Jess was entering her bedroom when Johnna said, "Goodnight, Jess. I hope you sleep well."

Jess paused, then responded, "Goodnight. You, too."

Johnna shut the door on a day that held potential—perhaps, even a promise that she prayed would be fulfilled in the days ahead.

Chapter 9

Lily stood and began collecting dishes from the breakfast table, as she declared: "All right, crew, time to get your jackets—hats and boots, if you have them. We're going to go exploring.

"What have you got in mind, Mom?" Johnna asked, unfastening Charlie from his booster.

"Well, we'll take the Jeep up the mountain to the ranger station, hike down to the Point, and let the children see the view of the valley—kind of 'get the lay of the land.' I've got snacks and iced water bottles packed in the Jeep if we need mid-morning recharging. There are a couple of picnic tables near the ranger station. Then, we'll ride down the river road past the old family cabin to the cemetery." Lily laughed, "We'll introduce the children to the kinfolk. Jess, your seven 'greats' back grandmother and grandfather are there—along with his second missus. I wonder how his first missus feels about that?" she laughed. "Then, we'll just keep on going down the road till we come out in Jasper and have an early supper at the 'all you can eat' restaurant there. How's that sound?"

"Like a plan!" Johnna declared. "I'll get little man ready," she added, removing the bib covering Charlie's favorite train shirt. "Jess, you might find some boots to wear in that basket in your closet - maybe just a bit loose, but not much." Lily was standing at the sink rinsing dishes, when Johnna said, "Jess is only eleven, and her shoes are just a half-size smaller than mine. I think she's going to have J. B.'s height."

Lily caught her breath for a moment and her vision blurred. Johnna had made a casual remark about J. B., without hesitation, without any suggestion of discomfort in the remembrance.

Jess, wearing the old hiking boots she had found in the closet basket, held Charlie's hand as they waited near the front door for their mother and grandmother. Lily appeared from her "add-on," as she called the annex that contained her private bedroom, bath, and office. Fritz was following close behind.

Charlie cried, "Fwitz" and pulled away from his sister, as Lily said, "Sit." Fritz sat and allowed himself to receive more hugs from the excited child and returned the affection with a wet lick. Charlie said, "Ooh, he kissed me again!"

Lily directed Fritz to stay, while she retrieved his orange armor vest from the seat of the hall tree. She began putting the dog's legs in the openings, and Charlie asked, "Fwitz's jacket?"

"Well," his grandmother replied, "it's a special vest that will protect him from briars and things that might be in the woods. It's a bright color too, so during hunting season people will know he's a dog, not a deer."

Johnna appeared from the guest bedroom, and Lily thought she looked like the college girl she was fifteen years ago—jeans, boots, the old olive pullover, and camo jacket she had found at the surplus store when she and her roommate went scavenging. Lily continued: "When we're in the woods, Fritz will walk ahead of us. If we see him stop and sit, we'll stop and be quiet, okay? He's telling us something is in our way, it's not safe to keep going, and we must wait until he says we can walk again. Okay?"

Charlie said, "Fwitz my friend. Him a good dog."

Jess corrected her brother: "He is a good dog, Charlie."

Charlie repeated, "He is a good dog."

Lily chuckled as she secured the straps across the dog's back, and Charlie said, "I like your jacket, Fwitz." He informed Jess, "His jacket orange, Jess."

"Yes," Jess replied. "That's right. What color is your jacket?"

Charlie looked down at his hoodie. "Wed and blue … and white!" running his finger across the stripe on his chest.

"Good job, Charlie!" Jess said.

Lily noted the enthusiasm with which Jess praised Charlie. "Charlie, your sister is a good teacher."

Jess replied, "Charlie is smart. He likes to learn. He knows his colors, he can count to twenty, and he knows the ABC song."

Lily said, "I won't be surprised if you have him reading before long. I have a good friend who is a teacher—she's very interesting. You might enjoy meeting her." She continued: "I think we're ready to be off. Johnna, we'll go out the annex door if you want to meet us around there with Charlie's car seat. The Jeep's parked at the side of the house. Also, I've got a child hiking carrier in there. We may have to take turns carrying Charlie when his little legs give out."

Chapter 10

A chill remained in the morning air, but there was promise of blue skies and the warm breath of springtime. Jess dreaded the sickening curves of the mountain road, but she had to admit the four-door Jeep made the ride exciting. Lily had not yet removed the soft top in anticipation of the summer months, but the vehicle still gave Jess a feeling of freedom and the thrill of an amusement park ride. Charlie continually bounced against the restraints of his car seat and clapped his hands. Occasionally, he would shout to the dog on guard behind him, "Fwitz, this fun!"

Turning off the main road at the top of the mountain, they passed through a small community of homes outside the game preserve. Her grandmother announced, "Children, many of these folks are your relatives. Your great-great aunt married a man up here on the mountain, and their family established this little settlement." Jess noticed a mixture of neat houses—well-preserved old ones, newer ones, all well-maintained. They passed by a yard with a border of old tires, painted white, buried half-way in the ground. There was also a tree that supported old boots made into hanging flower planters. Lily declared with a laugh, "I just love mountain landscaping and horticulture!"

At the entrance to the game reserve, they stopped at the ranger's station. Jess noticed her mother's strange expression as the ranger greeted Lily, "Hey there, Ms.

Craig! You're up and about early," and Lily responded, "Good morning, Luke. I've brought special visitors."

Jess noted the ranger was a tall, muscular man, with red hair and blue eyes. His boyish face had a pleasant smile for her grandmother, and Jess assumed they were friends.

"Luke, this is my daughter, Johnna, and her children, Jess and Charlie."

Charlie exclaimed, pointing behind him, "And Fwitz! My friend!"

Ranger Luke said, "Yes, sir, Charlie. Fritz and I are old friends, too. Well, good to meet you," he doffed his hat at Johnna and continued: "You have a good visit." With a wink to Lily, he warned, "Keep a watch out for unfriendly critters, Ms. Lily."

Putting the Jeep in gear, she replied, "We will. Thanks, Luke. If you like, join us for snacks later." Lily pulled away from the guard house toward the graveled parking area, where Jess noticed theirs was the only vehicle.

As they exited the Jeep, Jess heard her mom question Lily: "Luke? That would be Luke Ferguson?"

Her grandmother replied, "He's been a ranger up here for years—a great defender of the reserve and protector of people like us who come to enjoy it."

"He works here ... even after the accident?" Johnna asked. Jess assumed her mother must be referring to the situation that led to her brother Jeff's death.

Lily opened the tailgate for Fritz and retrieved the child carrier, as Johnna released Charlie from the car seat. "He's here to help—to do what he can when needed. He's qualified to be a wilderness first responder. He did that for a while out west, but he'd rather be here, where he grew up. There are few opportunities for heroics and glory,

31

thankfully, but he's got a mountain family who love him."

Lily attached a leash to Fritz's collar and handed Johnna the handle. "Just let Fritz take the lead—it's long. The rules say dogs must be on a leash. She placed the carrier on her back, buckled the strap around her, and said, "I'll carry Charlie down to the point and back. There are no guard rails."

"You sure you want to, Mom? He'll get heavy," Johnna asked.

"Sure, no problem. It's a piggyback carrier. He'll be able to stand so he can see over my head." She chuckled: "And, besides, he's all yours next time." Lily turned toward Johnna and gave instructions on securing Charlie to her back. Jess laughed at the cloudy expression of uncertainty on her brother's face and wondered if it would turn to tears. But, as soon as he felt safe and looked down at Jess from his new height, he exclaimed, "Charlie tall, Jess! Charlie tall!"

The path downward to the point was dry but rutted from the recent rains. They followed Fritz as he maneuvered around treacherous rocks and holes. It was a half mile through the forest before the trees separated to reveal they were standing on an enormous expanse of rock, a cliff looking over the "Grand Canyon of the Tennessee." There Fritz sat, stationing himself near the precipice, as if to warn them to go no farther. From their elevation, they could see the river, like a long, heavy snake wound around the foot of the opposite peak. Because of the curvature of the mountain on which they stood, below to the east they could see part of the roof of her grandmother's house. To the west, the river slithered away through the chain link of Appalachians to wend its way, Grandmother said, "To the Ohio, then to the Mississippi, then to the endless sea."

With a sigh, Johnna breathed the word,

"Beautiful."

Jess had to admit she had never seen a place like this. Grandmother said, "Jess, this is the land of your family for seven generations. Well, much longer than that, if you consider the women your ancestral grandfathers married were Cherokees. They were here long before the Scottish settlers arrived." Jess thought about the mountains in California. The ones she had seen were much taller, often snow-capped, majestic. But … something about these lush green peaks drew her to them— something warm, welcoming, almost familiar, as if they should be part of her memory. Considering what her grandmother had said, her father had felt it too. Jess imagined his voice: "If I had to be grounded, I'd be grounded here in these mountains." In her thoughts, Jess felt connected to her dad for brief, precious moments.

Charlie, who had piggybacked in silence, enjoying his vantage point, exclaimed, "Look!" and drew their attention to a bald eagle soaring above the trees below.

Lily remarked, "Aren't we the lucky ones to see him." They watched the bird sail and swoop before them, surely with sheer joy of being and realization of his magnificent appearance.

Jess thought about her dad and his soaring above the earth, like the eagle. How free he must have felt. She remembered part of the poem she had memorized for him—"I've topped the wind-swept heights with easy grace where never lark, or ever eagle flew." She knew in her heart her dad had looked down on the eagle, not from this rock or on this particular bird; but he knew the feeling of having "wheeled and soared and swung high in the sunlit silence."

Lily broke her reverie: "No wonder he's our national bird!" She continued, "Well, troops, how about we head back and get energized for our further adventures? I've got trail mix, apples, cheese and crackers, gingersnaps, and cold lemonade." Charlie agreed, "Let's eat!"

Chapter 11

The return trek uphill was tiring, and all but Charlie were breathless as their steps crunched across the graveled level to the Jeep. Lily directed Jess to get the basket between the seats and take it to the picnic table, while Johnna unstrapped Charlie and freed her mother of her load. Returning the carrier to the Jeep, Lily took out a bowl and said, "Johnna, I'm going to get Fritz some water at the ranger station, if you want to start unpacking the food."

Out of public view at the side of the Jeep, Johnna allowed Charlie his sudden urge to relieve himself, then dutifully cleaned his hands and face with baby wipes. As they walked to meet Jess, Charlie pulled away from Johnna's hand and ran toward the picnic table. Just as she warned, "Charlie, don't run," he stumbled and fell face down on the gravel, screaming in pain and fear. "Oh, no ... Charlie!" she shouted, as she ran to her son.

Johnna helped Charlie to his feet and saw blood running down his chin. Bits of rock and soil covered scraped arms and legs. "Oh, Charlie, baby!" she cried, as she brushed off dirt and called for Jess to bring a napkin. Soon, not only Jess and her mother were there, but also, Ranger Luke, carrying a first aid bag.

"Ma'am, do you mind if I take a look at him?" Luke asked Johnna.

"No ... no. Please. Thank you," she replied, as she

said, "Charlie, let Mr. Luke help you."

Luke was kind and gentle, as he said, "Charlie, first let's clean your face, so we can see where you are hurt." Luke carefully wiped Charlie's face with a wet cotton pad until he revealed the source of the blood. "Well, look at that—that's what I'd call a 'busted lip,' Charlie!"

The curious boy stopped crying and said, "A busted lip?"

"Yep," Luke replied. "Tough guys get busted lips all the time. You know the best thing for a busted lip?"

Charlie shook his head and sniffed, "No."

"Popsicles."

"Popsicles?" Charlie questioned, wiping tears with the back of his hand.

"Popsicles. Ms. Lily, would you mind getting me a popsicle from the minifridge in the shack? You like orange popsicles, Charlie?"

Charlie shook his head in agreement, as Luke cleaned the child's mouth with an antibiotic wipe, checked for loose teeth, and cleaned Charlie's arms and legs. "You know," Luke told Charlie, "You move too fast. You need to slow down, especially on gravel. You need to save the running for when you're playing ball or running in a race—times like that."

Charlie shook his head in agreement and took Luke's hand when the ranger asked, "You want to go to the picnic table and eat your popsicle?"

Johnna watched as her little boy walked next to the tall ranger. Lily, with the popsicle, met them at the table. Smiling, Johnna turned to Jess to meet an expression of rage and hostility. "Jess? What's wrong?" Something had triggered her daughter's upset, and Jess fled back toward the trail from which they had come, leaving her mother confused and questioning.

Johnna joined the others at the table and told her mother, "Jess is having one of her bouts of anger and has gone back down the trail."

Lily looked at Luke and asked, "Okay if I send Fritz?"

Luke responded, "Sure, it's just us up here today. Fritz is always on call of duty."

Lily released the clip on the leash and said, "Fritz, go. Find Jess." The dog ran toward the path to the point.

Chapter 12

Negative thoughts and feelings overwhelmed Jess' objectivity. Her head could "get" facts but had no control to sort and organize them rationally. Grief, fear, loss, change—what was real? Everything in her normal life had disappeared, leaving her feeling alone and lonely in a new, unfamiliar world she could not explain or understand—a world that could not understand her. Her mother wanted to move on, into a new life, but Jess could not extricate herself from the life that was. She was struggling alone, but she didn't know whether she was struggling to stay in her realm of solitude and memories or struggling to leave it to meet new companions and experiences. The visceral reaction she felt at the Point— the connection to her father, then Charlie's fall, the ranger's kindness, her brother's attachment to the man, her mother's smile as she watched them go hand-in-hand—it was all too much to process. As usual, she was angry at her mother, at her own confusion, and at a world that insisted on going on without her father—without Jess herself.

She was nearing the Point when Fritz intercepted the pathway and sat in front of her. "What do you want? Leave me alone! Go away!" she blurted at the immoveable animal.

"He'll not budge till he knows you've cooled down," came a voice from the rock. Jess saw a woman perched precariously on the edge of the cliff. Directing her words to the far side of the valley, she continued: "He's got more sense than most people I know, especially when they're not thinking straight."

For the moment, curiosity about this strange person quelled Jess' agitation. The woman was smaller than Jess—petite, dark braid hanging from a crumpled safari hat, denim jacket, brown corduroy pants, and weathered boots, swinging in childlike motion as they hung over the ledge. The woman turned toward Jess, revealing a poetically delicate and beautiful tanned face, from which drawled a grainy voice, heavy with mountain dialect. "Want to join me?" she asked.

"Who are you?" Jess asked defiantly.

"Calliope Winchester. Your grandmother calls me Callie. You ... may call me Calliope," she replied with an air of authority.

"Where did you come from? You weren't here a while ago," Jess declared.

"No, I'm here now. My cabin's down there near the road." She nodded toward the western treetops. "There's a trail runs up here from there." Calliope again turned her gaze to the far mountain and the river circling its feet. After a moment's standoff, Calliope continued, "Fritz will let you pass if you've pulled yourself together."

With thought, then a frustrated sigh of surrender, Jess said, "Okay."

Calliope said, "Fritz, come," and the dog moved toward the woman, who motioned him to lie down at her side but away from the rock's edge. "Now, you sit down back there, behind Fritz," Calliope ordered.

"How do you know Fritz?" Jess asked, as she sat cross-legged behind the dog's warm body.

"Fritz stays with me when Lily's away—the trips she's made to visit you ... the last time, when she went out there for your dad's memorial."

Jess hesitated, then asked: "Did you know my dad?"

"I met him once, before you were born. He and your mom hiked the trail up here to the Point. A handsome guy your dad … friendly. On the way back, they stopped at my place for a drink. We sat on the porch a while." Calliope paused and perused the landscape. "This place touched his heart, 'moved his soul,' were his words." She nodded to the creature still swooping from the height into the valley below. "He saw uwohali, the eagle. He said, 'Flying in a jet can't come close to the feeling of soaring over the valley like that bird.'"

"He loved California," Jess protested.

"He loved flying," Calliope rebutted, "and he loved these mountains. California was where he was able to do what he loved to do, but if given a choice ..." Calliope left the thought for Jess to finish.

Jess was silent, sorting memories in the light of the woman's words. Then, she stood and said, "I've got to go back. They'll want to leave soon."

"Fritz, go with Jess," Calliope ordered as she motioned to the dog. To Jess she said, "I'm just down the road a mile from your grandmother's house … when you want to talk."

Jess brushed off the seat of her pants and followed Fritz uphill to the picnic table. She frowned, wondering why this strange person would think she'd want to talk. As she topped the rise, she realized she was hungry and thirsty and hoped there would be food and drink left.

Chapter 13

Fritz ran ahead to his bowl and gulped water until the container was dry. Without a word, Jess approached the table. Her mother, Charlie, the ranger, and Grandma, engaged in conversation, were helping themselves to a spread of tempting snacks. Lily handed Jess a cup of icy lemonade and said, "Here you go. Bet you're thirsty. Have a seat," she gestured toward the space next to her. "Luke, pass a paper plate, please—down there," she pointed to the other end of the table. "Help yourself, Jess—there's plenty of everything. We'll pass what you can't reach."

Johnna found it challenging to ignore Jess' recent upset and to remain in her "new normal," in hopes of drawing Jess into it. Her mother had advised, "Don't go to her. Don't validate her choice of action. Be where your family needs to be—in a place of calm and stability. Let her choose to come to you. If nothing else, you can be your own calm port in her storm."

Johnna never doubted the wisdom of her mother's words, but it was agonizing to see Jess in pain. She wanted to take away the hurt and, in the process, heal her own. She had tried all the counselors had advised, all she could think to do … except … nothing … just do nothing. Lily had said, "Get yourself in a good place, a steady, comfortable place emotionally … and wait, with Charlie and with open arms, for her to join you."

Johnna appreciated Luke's interaction with her son, who, obviously, was soaking up the ranger's attention. Charlie winced at times, and the discomfort of his swollen mouth threatened tears. But Luke seemed to know how to distract the child from his injury, to focus him on a squirrel hopping nearby, to point out and identify various birds, to tell him about the forest animals he had seen.

The realization hit Johnna that she had been so concerned about what to do, where to go, how to manage—how to deal with Jess and her issues, that she, perhaps, had neglected the needs of her son and his growing mind and curiosity. Even in her volatile state, Jess had been a patient helper and teacher to him. Charlie—his innocence, his love, his joy, might be the place where mother and daughter could meet on common ground and begin to build "Normal."

"Johnna, do you mind if I take Charlie up to the ranger station?" Luke asked. "I've got some wildlife photos he'd like."

"Sure, thanks," she responded, glancing at Jess.

Luke added, "Jess, if you've finished eating, come with us. Charlie will be more at ease with you along, and I have information about the forest and our work you might find interesting."

Jess moved from her place, as Luke stood Charlie on the ground. The child went to his sister and took her hand, as he said through puffy lips, "Get Jess popsicle, Mr. Luke?"

The ranger replied, "I bet you'd like another one, too."

Even Jess laughed when Charlie answered, "Uh-huh, for busted lip."

Johnna watched the trio go toward the ranger station, a neat log structure, having, as Lily described, an office area behind the visitor's window and an adjoining bunk room with private shower bath. "Luke stays up here at times" Lily said, "when the grounds have been closed to the public and he's covering a shift on the fire tower." Lily pointed out the portable toilet for the public at the edge of the graveled parking area. "That's the worst part of their job, I'd say—keeping that place clean." Lily declared, "People can be thoughtless, nasty creatures."

Johnna replied with a wink: "Well, I'm about to find out if they have been naughty or if the ranger has been nice."

Lily laughed, "I'm right behind you." She turned to Fritz, who was resting in the shade of the picnic table. "Fritz, come." She advised her daughter, "Always let Fritz take the lead when you're out and about up here." She motioned for the dog to precede them.

Only a couple of yards from the portable toilet, Fritz sat, and Lily whispered, "Stop, Johnna." In their silence, they heard the warning rattle, emanating from the facility under logs that leveled its foundation. Never had Johnna heard the sound, but now she would never forget it. Surely her mother could hear Johnna's heart pounding in her chest—it was pulsating through her whole body.

After two minutes that seemed to Johnna like two hours, Fritz moved toward the portable toilet and circled it. Then, he came back to Lily giving her the cue to proceed.

"We can go on now," Lily said. "The snake's moved on."

"Mom, my knees are so weak they may not hold me."

Returning to the picnic table, Lily comforted her daughter, saying, "The snakes aren't aggressive unless frightened, so we just wait until one decides to be on his way. Those are the 'critters' Luke warned us about when we came in the reserve. Somebody got the bright idea to introduce rattlers into the state forest—they're endangered species, don't you know? So, now, if not careful, we humans are endangered when we meet up with one—or five hundred dollars poorer if we get caught doing away with it."

"Oh, mom, what if it were Jess or Charlie running up on a rattler?"

"Let's ask Luke to talk to them about snakes ... and identifying poison oak ... about just general forest safety. They would listen and learn from him as an authority—nothing to frighten them, just to prepare them. Then we could ask them to teach us what they've learned, to confirm they've got it ... boost their confidence ... give them a sense of responsibility."

Johnna pondered her mother's words as they put away the food and cleaned the picnic table. Lily threw Fritz the remaining crackers and poured melted ice from the cups into his bowl.

They loaded the Jeep and walked to the visitor's reception window at the ranger's station, where they viewed Luke sitting in a desk chair with Charlie on his lap and Jess standing at his shoulder. Luke was showing them an album of nature photos he had taken in the forest and was explaining the meaning of flora and fauna. Lily knocked on the window. Luke stood, handed Charlie to his sister, and said, "Jess, you sit here with Charlie. The captions tell you what you're seeing, so you can explain them to him."

Luke went to the window and asked, "You ladies about ready to head out?"

Lily responded, "Yep, going to look for another adventure." Lowering her voice, she added, "We just had our first."

There was a question on Luke's face, as he asked, "One of our critters?"

Directing her words to her grandchildren, she asked, "Are you children learning about the forest and its animals?"

"Yes, ma'am," Jess responded."

Charlie pointed at a picture in the album and said, "This a waccoon. I like waccoons."

Johnna said, "As soon as you're finished, we're ready to do more exploring, okay?"

Charlie nodded, turning his attention back to the album, and Jess said, "Okay."

Lily motioned for Luke to come outside the station away from the children. "It came from the crossties under the portable toilet. Fritz warned us and stood him off. He was a good sized one, from what little I could see—and hear. Luke, maybe next time you're at the house, you can talk to the children about their safety in the forest. We don't want to frighten them, but they need to know how to watch out for 'critters' and things that come right down on our property."

"Sure thing. How about I bring some materials by Sunday afternoon?" he suggested.

"If you'll come for Sunday dinner beforehand," Lily replied.

"I was hoping you'd ask, Ms. Lily," he laughed.

"Since when do you need an invitation?" she retorted.

"Well, not so much an invitation, as checking to see if you've got room for one more with your family here."

Lily said, "Luke, you are family."

"Thank you, Ms. Lily. You know you're about all

I've got … except Callie, of course. But you know Callie …"

"Oh, yes, and I love her, too, but she's not what they call 'a people person.'"

The children joined them, and Charlie whined, "I don't want to go."

Johnna said, "Charlie, Mr. Luke is coming to eat dinner with us Sunday, and he's going to bring some more pictures for you. We'll see him soon. Can you say 'Thank you' to Mr. Luke? He took good care of you today."

Charlie took Luke's hand again and said, "Thank you, Mr. Luke."

Johnna looked at Jess, who added, "Yes, thank you."

Luke responded, "I enjoyed your visit. Thanks for sharing your snacks. You all be safe, and I'll see you Sunday."

As they loaded the Jeep and headed out of the reserve, Luke was standing at the door of the station. He waved as they passed by and yelled, "Pot roast!" Lily laughed and gave him a "thumbs-up." Johnna concluded that Luke Ferguson was a very nice first addition to her circle of friends in "Normal."

Chapter 14

Jess, eager to get out of Sunday clothes and into jeans, was close behind her grandmother as they entered the house. She had to admit the group of young people in the Bible class were friendly, and the sermon was one she could understand—"The Inside of the Cup," as announced in the bulletin—about the "outside" of a person looking and acting lovely, while the hidden "inside" might be truly stained and ugly. Jess was uncomfortable as the preacher spoke about hypocrisy, but then she thought, I haven't been hypocritical—I've been acting like I feel—rotten!

Her grandmother called, "Johnna, when you and Jess get changed, how about setting the dining room table? And move Charlie's booster in there, too."

"Sure, Mom," Johnna replied, "as soon as I get Charlie into his play clothes."

Jess had entered the kitchen when the doorbell rang, and her grandmother asked, "Jess, would you get that, please?"

Jess found Luke Ferguson on the porch, a thick portfolio in one hand and a handled carrier in the other. Seeming unsure of his direction, he concluded: "I'm just going to put this over here," and settled the crate in the shaded corner nearest the door. Entering the house, he smiled and greeted Jess, "Hello, again." Handing her the portfolio, he said, "You want to put these on the coffee table till after dinner?" Jess accepted the folder and moved toward the living room area, as Luke said, "Thanks."

"Luke, in the kitchen," called Lily. As he entered, she questioned, "Since when do you have to ring the bell?"

"Since I had my hands full, Ms. Lily," he laughed. "We're going to have our safety and identification class after dinner—until Charlie's nap time."

"I don't want to take a nap," Charlie whined, as he followed Luke into the kitchen.

"Hey, buddy," Luke turned to face the small figure behind him. "You snuck up on me!"

"I don't want to take a nap," he repeated.

"Well, that's what we guys do after a big Sunday dinner." He said, "I have a surprise for you, if you promise to take a nap after we look at the pictures I brought."

"Okay, I take a nap," Charlie said smiling.

"Charlie, go wait with Jess while we get the food on the table. We're moving hot food," Lily directed.

Johnna, twisting her hair up and securing it with a comb, entered the kitchen. "Hey, Luke. Okay, Mom, give me my marching orders."

"Johnna, get the good dishes and glasses from the cabinet next to the fridge. You know where the silverware is. Placemats and napkins are in the credenza—oh, and a hot pad for the table." As she finished arranging the pot roast and vegetables on a platter, she said, "Luke, you can take this out and set it on the hot pad."

Accepting the dish, Luke responded, "Oh, there is nothing better than the smell of your pot roast."

"Hope you enjoy it," Lily replied. "And I've got your favorite peach cobbler and ice cream for dessert."

"Wow, it can't get any better!" he exclaimed.

As Jess watched the activity around the dining table, her mother chimed in: "It'd be better if she'd take all the calories out!"

Luke responded, "Calories don't count on Sundays … or holidays, birthdays, game days, et cetera, et cetera." He grinned as he added: "Besides, they don't seem to be doing you any damage."

Jess noticed her mother's cheeks flush, as Johnna replied, "It takes a couple of weeks, I hear, for the calories to show up on the body. About a week from Friday, I'll be bulging." Jess felt the anger swelling inside her, and she fought to stay in control of her emotions. The familial banter of her mother with Luke Ferguson seemed an insult to the memory of her father. She thought, *Am I the only one who remembers Dad—the only one who cares?*

Lily called, "All right, we're ready. Jess, you want to get Charlie into his seat?"

Jess picked up her brother, fastened him into the booster, and Fritz crept close, ready to clean up falling crumbs. Unable to hide her expression of displeasure and avoiding eye contact with her mother and Luke opposite her, she sat in the chair next to Charlie and waited as he said the blessing: "Thank you, God, for our food … for Grandma, Mama, Mr. Luke, and Sissy … for Fwitz … and for Charlie! Amen."

"Thank you, Charlie," said his grandmother. "You are becoming such a fine little man. Did you enjoy your class this morning?"

If Jess had not been so hungry, she might have made a petulant exodus to her bedroom. The exuberant conversation of fellowship around the table irritated her, while making her feel alone in her world of determined resistance to joy. She ate her food in silence, as her thoughts whirled like gravel in a dust devil—until her ears picked up her grandmother's reference to Calliope. Lily asked, "Have you seen much of Callie lately, Luke?"

"No, she's been keeping to herself. She's in

reclusive mode now that she's between semesters."

"I remember Calliope," Johnna stated. "She lived in that cabin on the trail up to the Point. J. B. and I met her when we were hiking years ago."

Lily replied, "She's still there. You remember I mentioned Jeff had a serious girlfriend, those months before the accident?"

"Yes. I recall your saying he was thinking about settling down," Johnna replied.

Lily said, "Yes, with Callie, Jeff's sister—in that cabin."

"Well, she's my half-sister," Luke clarified. "My dad died of an aneurysm when I was about Charlie's age, and my mom married my stepfather when I was four. I couldn't have asked for a better dad. He loved me as much as he loved Callie—Calliope, who was born a year after they married."

Jess was a sponge absorbing details about Calliope and her relationship to Luke and even to her own Craig family. Questions were popping into her mind, but she couldn't ask them without stepping out of her self-imposed isolation. Curiosity threatened to break down her defenses.

"You said she's between semesters?" Johnna queried.

Luke answered, "She teaches English and literature at the college. Between semesters, she holes up in that cabin and doesn't socialize much—hasn't in years now."

"Losing Jeff was hard for all of us," Lily said, as she placed her hand on Luke's arm. "But part of Callie just shut down—shut off people, as much as she could and still survive."

"Yes," Luke agreed. "I moved back here, in part,

to keep a check on Callie. I stay upstairs at the cabin."

Johnna spoke up, "Mom, I have an idea. Why don't Jess and I take a plate of food to Callie? The guys are going to take their Sunday afternoon naps, and we could get a little exercise by walking down to the cabin and back."

"Why, I think that would be a fine idea—don't you, Luke?" Lily asked.

"Well, sure. She's not unfriendly, just quiet … 'into herself' at times. She'd have to welcome your food, Ms. Lily." He added, "I have an errand to run before my nap. Just make sure you leave leftovers for Charlie and me after naptime, right Charlie?"

Charlie nodded. "And Fwitz?"

"Right," Luke said, "and Fritz."

Chapter 15

Johnna watched as Luke showed the children the identification guides, and she was thankful for the review of things that lay hidden in her mind, under the accumulation of adult tasks, responsibilities … and memories. He was saying, "If you think a plant may be poison oak, just don't touch it. There are three leaves growing off the stem, and the leaves look like the leaves of the oak tree—see here. Also, there are little thorns growing on the stems. In the spring, poison oak will have light green berries, then, little flowers until fall, when the leaves turn a red orange. Now, this is poison ivy …"

Johnna appreciated Luke's patience with the children and his concern for the knowledge that would equip them for living near the forest. As a child, she had roamed the mountainside and woods without any concern for safety and, by the grace of God, had suffered no injury except the occasional rash. As a mother, she valued the freedom of childhood exploration, but she was aware of the potential for harm. She wanted Jess and Charlie to have an affinity and curiosity for nature in what, she was concluding, would be their new home—at least for the immediate future. She needed to be here, near her mother, near her roots, in the security of wisdom and stability, in the comfort of memories without barbs to the soul.

Luke concluded his lesson with the intriguing words, "Okay, kids, I have a surprise. Come out on the porch." He looked at Johnna and Lily, sitting in the nearby armchairs, and nodded toward the porch, motioning for them to join them.

Collecting the carrier from the corner near the house, Luke took gloves from under the handle and slipped them over his hands. He asked, "Charlie, can you be quiet and still?" Luke reached into the crate to retrieve the ball of fur that was making its home there.

Charlie nodded, then whispered, "A waccoon, a waccoon!" His arms trembled as he restrained his enthusiasm to bounce.

Johnna noticed Jess could not deny a smile, as Luke held the creature and said, "This is Bat Girl. I call her that because of her mask. Her mother was killed when she was hit by a car. My sister and I have kept her over the weekend, but she's ready to go to the rehabilitation center. I thought you'd like to see her first."

"I pet her?" asked Charlie.

"No, sorry, Charlie. We have to avoid contact with people as much as possible. That's why I'm wearing gloves. This is the only time she's been out of the carrier since I found her near her mother's body. "When I leave here, I'm taking her to the people who can legally care for her."

"I love her," Charlie whispered. "She beautiful."

Luke gently eased the raccoon back into the carrier. "She'll get checked out and get food and water. Before long, hopefully, she'll go back to live with other raccoons in the forest." He added, "Jess, you and Charlie keep the nature pictures for a while, so you can review them." Turning to Johnna and Lily, he continued: "Ms. Lily, thanks for the great meal, as always. Johnna, it was a pleasure to be with you."

Charlie wrapped his arms around Luke's leg and

said, "Mr. Luke, you stay."

Jess pulled her brother away from the ranger, as Luke said, "Charlie, I need to get Bat Girl to the people who can take care of her, as soon as possible. Now, you go take that nap you promised. I'll take Bat Girl, then take a nap myself, and come back for those leftovers with you. Okay?"

Charlie responded with a pout and a reluctant, "Okay."

Luke picked up the carrier and said, "See you ladies later," then made his way to his truck.

Johnna said, "Okay, young man, let's get you settled." She added, "Mom, can you keep an eye on him while Jess and I take that walk?"

Lily replied, "Sure thing. I'll just curl up with him, and we'll read until we both go to sleep. How's that, Charlie?"

"We read Wild Things," he declared.

"Yes, we'll read Wild Things," Lily laughed.

Chapter 16

The road's previous gravel surface, now paved, was still narrow, allowing only two cars to pass in opposite directions, with no shoulder for pedestrians. Thankfully, Johnna noted, this stretch of road was long curves with good sightlines—they would see or be seen in time by any approaching vehicle. Johnna ended their uncomfortable silence, asking, "You don't mind my suggesting this visit?"

Jess did not respond.

Johnna continued: "I hope we can brighten Callie's day. Grandma's roast and cobbler surely have brightened mine."

Again, Jess had no words, except, Johnna thought, vengeful, hateful ones threatening to tumble out to pierce her mother for injuries neither of them could identify.

Johnna stopped and spoke directly to her daughter: "Jess, I love you more than life itself, but I am tired—tired of trying to get through whatever wall it is you have built between us. I loved your father, but I am not responsible for his death. If there is any blame, it's his ... but I don't fault him for loving what he did. He loved flying, and it was his choice to risk his life—and the family we had, to do what he loved." Johnna began walking again. "I now need to be here, at home—in this place your dad and I enjoyed, a place he loved ... but not more than flying. I want a happy, normal life, where we can speak about your dad with love and ease, just like Grandma and Luke speak about the loved ones they've lost. Your dad can be part of our life, our peace and happiness, but we must get rid of anger … and stop assigning blame and guilt for something only your dad could control."

They neared the path to the cabin, and Jess spoke: "He saw uwohali, the eagle."

Johnna, blinking back tears, asked, "Uwohali? How do you know?"

"I knew when I saw the eagle … I felt it … and Calliope told me he did."

"You've met Calliope?"

"I met her when I went back to the big rock. She told me about meeting Dad when you went hiking … before I was born."

Johnna pondered the information Jess had shared, with silent thanks for the blessing of her sharing it.

Leaving the road, they followed the path to the cabin. An old steel blue Forester was parked near the porch, where Calliope was sitting in a rocking chair. Without speaking, she nodded at her visitors. Johnna announced them: "Calliope, you may not remember me. I'm Lily Craig's daughter, Johnna McGregor, and this is my daughter, Jess. I think you two have met."

"Yes," Calliope answered, "up at the Point."

"We've brought you a plate of food from Mother's Sunday dinner. As usual, it's very good, and she made enough for an army."

"Thanks. That's neighborly of you," she responded. "Come inside. I'll put that in the refrigerator." Johnna and Jess followed her into the cabin, allowing the screen door to slam shut behind them. Stairs to their immediate right took their eyes up to the loft that loomed over them.

"Have a seat," Calliope directed, indicating the sofa located before the fireplace in the open expanse before the eat-in kitchen.

Making conversation, Johnna said, "Luke says you are between semesters at the college."

"I have a couple of weeks before summer school begins. Then I only have one class until fall."

"I guess you enjoy the break and some down time." Johnna's eyes swept the cabin's interior. "This is a nice cabin," she observed. "Well-designed."

"That was Jeff's doing," Calliope offered. "He wanted it to be 'our alpha and omega home,' he said."

Johnna smiled softly. "He was going to be a fine architect."

"He was a fine architect," Calliope corrected. "He didn't need a degree to prove it."

Calliope noticed Jess' interest in the photographs on the fireplace mantle. "Help yourself to a look-around. I'm a simple person with a simple, yet not uninteresting, home."

Chapter 17

Jess looked at the photographs on the mantle—a younger, happier Calliope, petite and delicately beautiful, next to her Uncle Jeff, his arm wrapped around her narrow waist ... Jeff and Luke, their hands linked, making a seat for Calliope on their outstretched arms—ankles crossed, she looked pert and pretty between the two men in her life ... Jeff and Calliope sitting on the top porch step of the cabin, the forest around them awash in the colors of autumn.

Calliope pointed to the framed artwork bordering the living area. "Those are architectural drawings Jeff did. He won an award for the design back there between the office and the bedroom."

Jess moved around the room as she followed the succession of drawings. When she came to the bedroom, she noted the door was partially open, revealing a monastic arrangement of a single bed, with a bookstand lamp table and bedside chair. The drawing near the door was an impressive rendering of the façade of a "Cultural Arts Center," with amphitheater, art gallery, coffeehouse, and a shop featuring imported gifts and collectibles.

The door on the other side of the drawing was open, revealing Calliope's office, a room as abundant in the stuff of literature and professorial pursuits as the bedroom was sparse. Interrupted by a window in each wall, ceiling height bookcases surrounded the part of the room Jess could see. Volumes, neatly arranged and catalogued, filled the shelves; and planted in their midst was a long worktable with room for a computer, stacked divider shelves, pencil and pen holder, and ample workspace that currently held books—closed, opened, stacked, and a pile of large note cards.

Without thought of intrusion, Jess stepped into the comfortable isolation of the room. She wondered if it was the study itself that gave a feeling of contentment in studious solitude, or if it was Calliope's own disposition lingering in the atmosphere of the room.

"Jess, are you ready to head back?" her mother called, standing to move toward the door.

Jess responded, "You ought to see Uncle Jeff's drawings before we go."

"Show her, Jess," Calliope said.

Jess led her mother around the room to the drawing of the arts center, where Johnna stopped and sighed. "I see Jeff in this drawing—the subject, the colors, the light. It's elegant, classic, yet with a contemporary vibe.

Calliope joined them. "You know your brother well."

"Not as well as I would have liked," Johnna admitted. "Well, come Jess. We need to get back before Charlie wakes up … and let Calliope have some time before Luke comes back for his nap."

"He won't come back until tonight," she informed them without explanation, as Johnna moved toward the door.

Calliope again said, "Come back, Jess, when you want to talk."

Jess frowned as she questioned the strange implication of Calliope's words. *Why would I have any desire, any need, to talk to you?*

Chapter 18

"And the wild things roared their terrible roars and gnashed their terrible teeth and rolled their terrible eyes and showed their terrible ..." Charlie's head slumped against Lily's chest, as he lay in the crook of her arm. How sweet to feel the warmth and innocence of his body. There had been little opportunity to cuddle with three-year-old Jess like this. Johnna and J. B. hardly seemed to land at one base before the Air Force was moving them to another. She and John had visited them at Eglin when Jess was born, before John became too ill to travel. How I miss him. He would have enjoyed Charlie so much.

Lily carefully closed the book and scooted Charlie's sleepy head onto the pillow. She had placed him on the bed in her room, where Fritz remained nearby. She wanted to ensure the bond between boy and dog grew strong.

Kneeling next to the bed, Lily reached under the skirt to feel for the plastic crate. Occasionally she perused its contents and reflected on the memories inherent in them: Johnna and Jeff's baby shoes ... John's billfold and pocket watch ... his favorite ties, still smelling of the "Obsession" cologne she had given him ... Johnna's "Doll-Doll," made ragged by rough love, its hair stiffened by sticky baby fingers ... and there, her specific goal— Jeff's first denim barn jacket. Lily had laundered it and folded it carefully in tissue before putting it away with memories of her young son, who grew stronger and worked harder whenever he put on the jacket that was "just like Daddy's." Lily held it up to assess its condition—just a bit of wear—and the right size for Charlie to get a couple of years' use. She returned the lid to the container and pushed it back under the bed. While Charlie finished his nap, she would press the jacket and hang it up for him to try when Johnna and Jess returned.

Lily put away the clothes and pillowcases she had ironed and hung the jacket on Johnna's bedroom door. She was returning the ironing board and iron to the pantry when Johnna and Jess came into the kitchen. "We're back," her daughter declared, "and ready for some cold lemonade if you've got it."

"Sure, help yourself," Lily replied. "How was your visit?"

"Cordial. Calliope sends thanks for the food. She's not a big talker but pleasant enough." Johnna and Jess sat at the table with their glasses, as Johnna continued, "She lives with photos of Jeff and his drawings all around her."

"I know," Lily sighed as she joined them. "She can't seem to move on with her life. If not for her teaching and the little interaction she has with Luke and me, she'd be a complete recluse."

"What about men ... dating? She's still a young woman. It seems she'd want her own family."

"You'd think so," replied Lily. "She's obviously an attractive person, and I'm sure she's had opportunities. But ..." Lily considered her words: "Callie lost part of herself when Jeff died. She finds comfort and satisfaction amid her books." Lily swirled the lemonade in her glass. "She's as close to me as anyone, I think because I'm her link to Jeff. If I can't motivate her, I don't know who can." She stood to gather the glasses and put them in the sink.

"By the way, I had Jeff's barn jacket he wore like a uniform when he was about Charlie's age. It's clean and pressed. I hung it on the bedroom door for him."

"Thanks, Mom. He'll enjoy that. I guess he's still napping?" Johnna asked.

"Yes, back on my bed, with Fritz. He was asleep before the wild things roared their terrible roars for the third or fourth time!" she laughed.

Johnna said, "He never gets tired of that book. I'll just peek in and check on him."

Lily said, "Jess, I'm just going to wash these glasses by hand, if you don't mind drying and putting them away." The one she was holding crashed into the sink, when her daughter screamed, "Mom! Jess! No! Charlie! He's gone!"

They found Johnna standing next to the wrinkled bed. There was no Charlie, no Fritz, and the annex door to the outside was open.

Chapter 19

The frantic women raced out the door calling Charlie's name. Lily directed Jess to look around the house, then to go up the hill to the mini barn.

"Call Fritz, Mama!" Johnna urged. "He'll come if you whistle."

"No, we don't want him to leave Charlie. Fritz will do what he can to protect him." Lily added, "Charlie can't have gotten far—his little legs will wear out on this slope—besides, it's been only minutes."

The roar of Luke's truck engine growled to a stop as he pulled up behind Lily's Jeep. Jumping from the cab, he asked, "What's going on? I saw you as I came back into the clearing."

"Charlie's gone," Johnna sobbed. "I'm going to check in the garage." With a hopeful thought, she added, "And back in the house. Maybe he didn't go out. Maybe he's still in the house." She raced back up the steps into the annex.

Lily turned to Luke and said, "I really feel he's out here somewhere. Fritz is with him. But we've heard nothing from them—no barking, no crying, nothing. Jess is checking out the mini barn."

"I'll go up the hill," he replied. "Why don't you go over to the creek—make sure Charlie's not playing there."

Lily tried to suppress the feelings of fear and guilt threatening her composure. She had to remain calm to deal with the task at hand—finding Charlie and helping Johnna and Jess through the trauma of what, she prayed, would be only the after-effects of what might have been.

The creek running along the boundary of the property was a shallow rapids after the recent rains. Lily could see its course flowing toward the road—but no Charlie or Fritz, so she began hiking upstream.

"Lily, come quick! Johnna, Jess, I've found them!" Luke shouted. "Up here at the big rock."

When the women came in sight of the boulder projecting from the hillside, they saw Charlie toddling down the hill as fast as his legs could move. Behind him, Luke carried Fritz. Jess, with Johnna close behind, was the first to catch Charlie before he tumbled down the hillside.

Luke continued toward his truck. "Lily, put down the tail gate. We've got to get him to the emergency vet."

"Jess, get the blanket from my bed and my purse on the dresser," Lily ordered.

"What happened?" Johnna asked, taking her crying child from Jess' arms.

"Snake bite," Luke responded. Charlie ran up on the rattler behind the big rock. He knew to be still and quiet, but he was too close. Fritz got between Charlie and the snake and took the hit.

Jess returned with the purse and blanket. In the truck bed, Lily spread the cover, Luke laid the dog on it, and Lily hopped in beside him before Luke closed the gate. "You know you're not supposed to ride back here," he warned her.

"Try to stop me," she demanded.

Luke pushed his truck as fast as the law and the old engine would allow, to shorten the twenty-minute drive to the clinic. Lily knew the race against time was not in their favor. Even though Fritz had been vaccinated against rattlesnake bite, he had not received a booster—besides, she knew vets disputed the effectiveness. Fritz was alert but drooling and in pain. At best, he might survive days of agony and specialized treatment. From what she could see, the puncture was closer to his shoulder than to his heart; and she prayed that, on this Sunday afternoon, traffic would be light. Lily tried to calm and soothe Fritz, gently stroking his head, as she silently thanked him—*Fritz, you saved Charlie. You are our hero.* She knew it was her imagination; but, as he rolled his eyes to look at her, she thought she saw ... what? ... affection? Yes, but more than that ... satisfaction of a job well-done, a purpose fulfilled? She knew she would do all within her power to save this dog, to heal him and make him comfortable. If her efforts failed, he would receive a hero's burial. *You saved my grandson*, she thought, kissing his head.

Chapter 20

"Jess, get me the package of wipes from the bathroom." With Charlie sobbing on her lap, Johnna sat on the edge of the bed in the guest room. Pressing his body against her, she declared, "Charlie, never ever do that again! Never go outside by yourself!"

Charlie struggled to speak, choking on his words, sniffling, and wiping away tears. "Big snake ... big snake ... I was quiet ... Mr. Luke said, 'Be still.'" His sobs intensified with the recollection of his fear.

Jess sat next to them on the bed, as Johnna took wipes and began cleaning Charlie's face and hands and the scratches on his arms and legs. "Charlie, never go outside without a grown-up with you."

Charlie choked, "Waccoon ... I find a waccoon."

Johnna looked at Jess and shook her head in exasperation. "You let Mr. Luke help you with that."

Charlie sat up. "Fwitz? Where Fwitz?"

Jess answered, "Grandma and Mr. Luke took Fritz to the doctor. The snake bit him."

Trying to ease her son's resurging upset, Johnna added, "The doctor will give him a shot to make him better."

Through new tears, Charlie blubbered, "Him a good dog. Fwitz my friend."

Johnna agreed, "Oh, yes, Charlie, Fritz is a very good dog ... a very good friend."

Johnna again pulled Charlie against her. She wrapped a free arm around Jess, who allowed herself to be drawn close to her mother's shoulder. Fear, loss, potential tragedy had brought the three of them together like this—how sweet it felt, Johnna thought. A fearsome snake and a fearless dog friend seemed to have accomplished more in minutes than anyone or anything else had in months, even years.

Chapter 21

The aftermath of the adrenaline surge left Jess tired, but she sensed her emptiness was beginning to fill with something solid and real. The closeness with her mother felt good—something she had missed without realizing it, something she had needed, yet denied and avoided. Charlie's disappearance had frightened her beyond words; but every other person in her small yet expanding world had shared that fear—her mother, Grandma Lily, even Ranger Luke. Still, they had worked together, with unity of purpose, to search for Charlie and, she knew, like herself, to pray he was not injured—or worse. Fritz, just a dog, as intelligent and well-trained as he might be, had been their only hope for Charlie's protection; and the dog had proven himself trustworthy and loyal, risking his own life for that of his small ward.

The McGregor trio stayed huddled together until Charlie raised his head and questioned, "When Fwitz come back?"

Johnna glanced at Jess and replied, "I'm not sure, Charlie. The doctor may want to keep Fritz in the hospital a few days to make sure he is completely well. A snake bite can make a dog very sick."

"Make Charlie sick too," he declared. "Mr. Luke said, '"Be quiet. Don't move, till the snake go away.'"

"That's right, Charlie." Johnna pulled him close again. "I'm so glad you remembered what Mr. Luke told you. You are such a smart boy."

Jess asked, "Mom, why don't I get us some ice

cream?" She suggested, "Maybe that would make us all feel better and take Charlie's mind off ... you know... things."

"That's a great idea," she responded, setting Charlie on his feet. "Come on, son, let's go to the kitchen, and Jess will get us some ice cream."

Jess spooned ample scoops into three bowls, garnished each with one of Grandma's gingersnaps, and placed them on the kitchen table. Johnna buckled Charlie in his booster seat and sat at her own place. Johnna laughed: "Wow, look at this ice cream. Jess, I declare you the official scooper from now on. What do you think, Charlie?"

"Umm, lots of ice cream." Jess distributed spoons and paper napkins and took a seat at the table, as Charlie continued, "I say prayer."

Johnna agreed, "Sure, Charlie. You say a prayer." Johnna and Jess bowed their heads. As Jess peeked to see Charlie as he prayed, she caught her mother peeking also, and they shared a precious smiling moment.

"Dear God," Charlie said, "Thank you for ice cream. Thank you for Fwitz. Please make him better. Thank you for Mama, Jess, Grandma, and Mr. Luke. ... and thank you for cookies. Amen."

They enjoyed their ice cream in silence, before Johnna asked, "Charlie, how old are you?"

Charlie didn't stop eating but held up his free hand with two fingers.

"That's right," his mother responded, "But in about a week you will be one year older. How old will you be then?"

Charlie finished his last bite of ice cream, wiped his mouth with the napkin, held up three fingers and said,

"Fwee!"

Jesse exclaimed, "That's right, Charlie! That's so good!"

Johnna agreed, "Yes, very good, son." Directing her words to Jess, she added, "I know Charlie's a sharp little guy, Jess, but I also know how you've been working with him. You're doing a great job, and I appreciate that so much."

Jess paused, then replied, "Thanks, Mom. I love helping him. He has such a great memory and seems excited about learning."

Her mother's words were measured, as she responded, "You and Charlie are so much like your father ... in looks, of course ... but bright, inquisitive, always learning."

A moment of pain, then Jess looked down at the empty bowl in front of her and thought about the truthfulness of her mother's statement. Her dad was bright ... wanting to visit new places and learn new things ... sharing experiences with his children ... trying to teach them things he thought important. She remembered the time he tried to explain to her aerodynamics and how a plane weighing tons could stay in air weighing almost nothing. All she had learned was she didn't share his love or understanding of aviation. Jess could not restrain a smile, when Johnna continued: "Charlie also may have your father's daring, if today's raccoon hunting is any indication."

Johnna said, "Charlie, why don't you go play with your toys for a while before Grandma and Mr. Luke get back?" She released him from his booster seat and set him down to run away. When Charlie was out of hearing range, Johnna continued, "Jess, I was thinking we could have a birthday party for Charlie—nothing elaborate, just the three of us, Grandma, Luke, and maybe Calliope, if she would come. There were also a couple of children in his Bible class. We could invite them and their parents, so we all could make some new friends. What do you think?"

Jess considered her mother's suggestion, then answered, "Maybe we could have a Where the Wild Things Are party … have the kids wear pajamas, and we could make wild things hats and tails … have a Wild Things parade, a wild rumpus."

"That's a great idea. When we see how Grandma is doing, we'll talk to her about it. I know she has enough on her mind with the shock of Charlie's disappearance, though short-lived, and now, concern for Fritz." Her voice faded as she added, "I do hope he can survive this—and without damage."

As they sat together in silence, Jess knew the events of the afternoon replayed in their thoughts. Their lives could have been changed forever in a matter of minutes—an inquisitive child, an unlocked door, and more potential dangers than just the rattlesnake—falling on rocks into the creek, not being seen by a driver on the narrow road … Jess shook her head and sighed, "Mama, I'll go check on Charlie." She cleared the table and set their dishes in the sink.

"I'll wash those," Johnna offered.

"Thanks," Jess replied. She moved toward the doorway, then stopped and added, "You know, we ought to put high latches on the doors … just in case."

"Another good idea. I'll take care of that tomorrow. We need to return the rental car and scout out a vehicle of our own. You might have some ideas about what we need."

Jess was struck by the implication of permanence in her mother's words. Part of her still wanted to fight

change—the change of location, home, friends, school …
everything familiar, everything she had thought was tied
to J. B. McGregor. Yet, she could not deny she was drawn
to this place. What was it? … the knowledge of her father's
history here? … the feeling of his presence? … knowing
he, too, saw uwohali? Maybe this was where she was
meant to be. Maybe what happened to Charlie was proof
that providence was not only caring for a small child, but
relocating a stubborn, sullen girl—for her benefit and,
perhaps, for the good of others.

Charlie was playing on the bedroom floor with his
little people. She smiled as he sniffled and wiped his nose
on his arm. For now, he seemed to be calm, without fear.
Recalling her recurring nightmare of the explosion that
took her father's life, she feared the rattler would be a
returning threat to terrify Charlie and disrupt his sleep.

Chapter 22

Johnna heard Luke's truck as he pulled into the driveway, and she met him and her mother at the front door. Lily was disheveled and looked exhausted. Luke was carrying the blanket taken from Lily's bed.

Running from the bedroom, Charlie cried, "Fwitz! Fwitz!" as he and Jess joined them in the foyer.

Johnna asked, "What's the word on Fritz, Mom?"

"He'll have to stay in the hospital for treatment," she responded. "Let's go sit down, and I'll fill you in." She gestured toward the annex and said, "Luke, just throw that cover there in the hallway. I'll wash it tomorrow."

The four took seats in the living area, and Lily said, "Charlie, come sit on Grandma's lap." Lily hugged the child to her and asked, "Are you feeling better now, Charlie? I know you had a bad scare. We were all frightened when we didn't know where you were."

Charlie shook his head in agreement. "Big snake. Mr. Luke said be quiet."

"Yes, I know, and I am so glad Luke told you what to do—and you were smart enough to remember. That took a lot of courage." Lily kissed the top of Charlie's head and declared, "I'm so very proud of you. You are a brave little boy." Motioning to Jess, Lily said, "Charlie, go out on the front porch and rock while Jess reads you some stories."

Jess took her brother's hand and said, "Come on, Charlie, let's go pick out some books."

Watching the children exit the front door, Johnna asked, "Mom, what's the prognosis for Fritz?"

"Well, we got him to the emergency vet in good time, thanks to light traffic and Luke's heavy foot." She smiled and caressed Luke's arm as he sat next to her on the couch. "Our regular vet had given Fritz the rattlesnake vaccine. We don't know how much that will help, if at all. The vet cleaned the wound and immediately began a fluid drip with a vial of antivenom. He's also giving Fritz painkillers and antibiotics for infection. Thankfully, the strike was not in the heart, but close. He's very sick and uncomfortable. He's a big dog, so chances are he'll survive, but as far as permanent damage or aftereffects … we just won't know for a while."

With tears filling her eyes, Johnna replied, "I am so thankful for his being with Charlie." To Luke, she added, "And I am so grateful for the time you took with the children to safeguard them."

Luke said, "Charlie's one smart little guy. Not many his age would remember, much less in an actual encounter."

Lily declared, "We have a lot to be thankful for." She seemed to be struggling with her thoughts, then said, "Johnna, I am so sorry I had not locked the annex door. I never dreamed Charlie would go outside."

"Mom, please, don't feel bad about that. That could have happened to any of us—none of us would have thought Charlie would decide to go raccoon hunting," she smiled. "I'm going to put high latches on the outside doors. Tomorrow we're going to return the rental car and look for one of our own. I'll pick up latches while we're out."

Lily offered: "I'll follow you in the Jeep. You'll need transportation after you return the car."

Luke added, "I'll be on duty, but you can call my

cell if you need any advice on your car purchase." He laughed: "I know from the look of my old truck, you'd think I don't know much about cars and car trading, but you'd be surprised."

"Thanks, I'd appreciate the help. J. B. used to handle such things—I just drove whatever we had and knew to keep gas and oil in it. Beyond that, I'm ignorant," she answered.

"I'll steer you toward the reputable dealers," he continued, "where you can get a good used or program vehicle."

Johnna said, "Changing the subject ... before the kids come back inside ... Jess and I are thinking about having a birthday party for Charlie in a week or so, near his birthday. Would you mind, Mom?"

"Oh, I think that would be a fine idea. You just make the arrangements and tell me what you want me to do. The house is yours ... and I'll make the birthday cake," she added.

"Thanks, Mom. Luke, do you think Calliope would come?" Johnna asked.

He thought for a moment. "I just can't say for sure."

Johnna said, "Well, we'll give her a personal invitation."

Lily's voice trailed away, as she concluded, "I just pray Charlie's friend, 'Fwitz,' can be here for the celebration."

Chapter 23

Jess relished the freshness of the spring morning. The breeze rustling the trees, thick along the road, was just brisk and cool enough not to cause a chill. She was thankful her mother had allowed her this time and freedom to walk alone to Calliope's cabin. As a girl, her mother had roamed the wooded slopes and walked the riverside without fear. After Charlie's encounter with the snake, Jess suspected Johnna struggled against all kinds of fearful scenarios involving her children and the potential dangers of their new location.

Though Johnna had not said it outright, Jess knew this valley was going to be home—and, truthfully, she was beginning to hope so. They had been at Grandma's almost a week. So much had happened, so much was changing, yet, becoming more comfortable. Details of their future were unclear, but for now, Jess allowed herself to be disencumbered of negative thoughts and unanswered questions, to enjoy the luscious feeling of emancipation.

She had almost reached the path to Calliope's cabin, when she heard screeching coming from the river side. She picked up a fallen branch and cleared a path through the undergrowth to where the Tennessee was flowing—deep, forceful, and determined in its course downstream. As she turned toward a tall stand of evergreens, the source of the screeching, the eagle swooped down to seize a fish that seemed half the length of the awesome bird.

"Uwohali is having a late breakfast this morning." The voice of Calliope came from her position on the largest rock of a formation that tumbled into the river and around which the water splashed and gurgled. Calliope stood and made her way from rock to rock back to the bank. "You want to talk?" She passed by Jess without waiting for an answer and added, "Come with me."

Jess followed Calliope along a river trail that crossed the road and met the path to the cabin. She is odd, Jess thought, but interesting. The yard of the cabin was neat, but simply forest floor packed with the accumulation of years of leaf fall. Jess followed Calliope's example, who stomped her boots on the porch steps and wiped them on the mat before opening the door. Calliope directed, "Have a seat," as she hung her hat on a hook by the door. "Want some water? I've got that or fresh apple juice," she offered.

"Just some water would be good," Jess replied, again scanning the photos on the mantel.

Calliope handed Jess a glass of water and settled herself with a cup of coffee in the armchair near the fireplace. Jess waited for Calliope's next words, which did not come. Jess broke what seemed to her an awkward silence: "Calliope, Mom and I are planning a birthday party for Charlie, with just a few guests, in a couple of days. We'd like for you to come." When there was no response, she continued: "We thought it would be a good way to take his mind off the rattlesnake—I guess Luke told you what happened. He's having nightmares … and continually asking about Fritz."

Calliope replied, "Yes, bad business."

"Well," Jess continued, "Sunday afternoon, about three o'clock. There may be two other children from Charlie's Bible class. That would give them time for dinner and a nap before the party. What do you think? Will you come?"

Setting her cup on the chair side table, Calliope answered, "I'll think about it and give Luke my answer. He can tell you Sunday morning. Thanks for the invitation."

"You're welcome," Jess responded. Then, not knowing what more to say, she stood and said, "Well, I'll get out of your way."

"Want to talk?" Calliope asked.

Jess felt compelled to respond, "Why do you keep thinking I want to talk?"

Calliope shrugged. "Luke tells me you haven't been doing much of that lately."

"And you have?" she defended. "From what I understand you don't even talk to Luke much, and he lives here."

"'I love the stillness of the wood: I love the music of the rill: I love to couch in pensive mood upon some silent hill,'" came Calliope's eloquent words.

"What's that?" Jess demanded.

"Those are the words of a poet who found solace and peace in the voice of nature."

"So, what does that mean to me?" she argued.

"What does uwohali mean to you?"

"How do you know it means anything?"

"I don't … not for sure. But I suspect he does. He moved your father, and your father moves you."

"You know nothing about me or my father."

"'We have not wings, we cannot soar; but we have feet to scale and climb by slow degrees, by more and more, the cloudy summits of our time.' Longfellow. Your dad had wings, like uwohali. Some of us soar, and some of us plod along by slow degrees. Ultimately, we all reach the same destination, some sooner, some later. The task is finding our peace along the way."

Jess moved toward the door.

"Before you go," Calliope stopped her. "I have something for you. Come with me."

As she followed Calliope into her office, Jess wondered at the hold this strange, diminutive woman had on her. Perhaps it was nothing more than overwhelming curiosity that caused Jess to want to investigate, to know, to understand Calliope's eccentricity—at the same time, part of Jess wanted to flee Calliope's presumptuous intrusion into her soul.

Calliope's office, swathed in volumes of words and thoughts, again enveloped Jess in a feeling of warmth and comfort, even security. She watched as Calliope sat at the desk and retrieved a book from a lower drawer. "Here," Calliope said, handing Jess what appeared to be a journal, rich red, gold-embossed, with a magnetic flap closure. "I give each of my students one of these. This is an extra— for you."

"Thank you," Jess responded, "It's nice. But I'm not much of a writer."

"I believe you are," Calliope responded. "Write your thoughts and feelings on a page. Words give them form and texture—make them real. You can see them, assess them, discard them, or preserve them. They may give understanding of yourself not only to yourself, but to others, should you want to share your words and be understood."

Jess fanned the blank pages of the book before snapping the magnetic closure. She paused before intruding into Calliope's psyche: "Do you understand yourself?"

"A fair question," Calliope observed. "I do

understand myself, but I haven't shared that understanding with others—with no one since your uncle. 'The love of learning, the sequestered nooks, and all the sweet serenity of books,' she added, directing Jess' gaze to the shelves. With a faint smile, Calliope again said, "Longfellow."

"What was he like?" Jess was curious about the young man who understood Calliope and wanted to share his life with her.

"Who? Longfellow?"

Jess was surprised did gheat what must be a rare attempt at humor. She watched as Calliope leaned back in the desk chair, closed her eyes, and seemed to consider pursuing further conversation. Jess waited until she assumed there would be no answer and turned to leave, when Calliope's words stopped her: "He was grounded, practical, thoughtful ... but with a soul that could dream and the talent to make his dreams reality. While I was away at school, he bought and remodeled this cabin. When I came back to teach in Chattanooga, he brought me here and proposed as we sat out there on the steps. Luke came out from hiding to take our engagement picture—the one on the mantel. Jeff told me to move in—the place was mine. He said he knew I wasn't into diamonds—rather than put an engagement ring around my finger, he'd wrap this place around my heart." Calliope opened her eyes and sat up in her chair. "Jeff's effort at poetic symbolism. No Longfellow, but he got an A-plus for effort." Calliope's voice faded as she said, "He was staying with Lily until he passed his boards and we were married ... The wedding would be on Lily's porch ... about this time of year." Calliope stood and abruptly terminated the visit: "I'll let Luke know about the birthday party."

Amazed at Calliope's revelation of personal information and with her mind churning to put together the pieces of the puzzle that was Calliope, Jess let herself out the door and started toward home in the fading mist of morning. Her grandmother's house was in view, when the roar of an approaching car, speeding along the narrow road, caused her to move into the bushes and out of its way. Behind the wheel of the sleek, polished, surely expensive vehicle that passed her, she glimpsed the swarthy, menacing face of the driver. *Did he see me?* she wondered, knowing she would not forget his face and surely not wanting him to remember hers.

Chapter 24

Johnna finished setting the dining room table with the blue "ocean" tablecloth and, in the center, the toy ship approaching the wild things' "island"—a flat rock to which she had attached artificial foliage. From the ceiling she had hung vines all around the table area. Observing the completed setting, she thought, *Not bad, if I do say so myself.* At the head of the table, Charlie, in his crown as "king of all wild things," would sit, with a "wild thing" to his right and to his left. Johnna laughed to herself when she thought about the king and his subjects in booster seats and drinking from sippy cups.

Luke announced himself as he came in the front door: "Okay, I'm back. Ready for me to hang the banner?"

"Yes, sir," Johnna replied. "What do you think … maybe on the wall nearest the table?"

"Sure, and I'll hang it at wild thing level, so they can see it when they have their parade."

Entering from the guest room, Jess corrected Luke: "It's a wild rumpus, not a parade."

"Well, excuse me …wild rumpus. Sounds like a feral pig," he observed, making Jess laugh.

Handing Johnna a bag, Jess continued: "Charlie's still napping. Here are the claws, hats, and tails."

"Boy, this is going to be the neatest three-year-old's birthday party I've ever attended," Luke declared.

Johnna asked, "And how many have you attended?"

"Well, actually, this is the first," he replied.

Jess asked, "Is Calliope coming?"

"Well, she's been helping your grandmother and me with a birthday surprise. I've just come from the cabin. She'll make an appearance, at least for a few minutes."

Lily entered from the kitchen with a tray of cupcakes she set on the credenza. "Now, Luke, don't go spoiling our surprise."

"No way, Ms. Lily. I'm all about surprises," he laughed.

Johnna realized she was seeing a new aspect of Luke's personality—boyish, excited, eager to create a happy time for Charlie and his friends. *I should have bought claws and a tail for him*, she thought with a chuckle—*size extra-large*. Checking out the cupcakes, with wild things faces or with boats in blue seas of cream cheese icing, Johnna exclaimed, "Oh, Mom, these are great! The children will love them!"

"Thanks," Lily replied. "I've had fun making them."

"Well, it's about time for His Majesty to get up from his nap." Johnna turned toward the bedroom and tripped over Luke, who was still hanging banner low on the wall.

Catching her before either was damaged, Luke, face red with embarrassment, cried, "Whoa there!"

"Oh, Luke, I'm sorry. I forgot you were behind me." Flustered, she added, "Thanks for the save."

"No problem. Any time," he laughed.

Johnna noticed Jess was watching from her position next to Lily, and she was surprised when her daughter didn't react with displeasure, only curiosity, at her mother's interaction with Luke. Johnna was thankful Jess was not upset, didn't stalk off to sulk. She wondered if Jess ever would allow another man in their lives—in her mother's life. For sure, there would never be another J. B. McGregor, for either of them. But could there be another someone, special in his own way, who might mend their broken hearts and find room in them for the healing he brought?

Luke stood and said, "Okay, ready for the rumpus. Johnna, I'm going to go check on that surprise. I'll be back before the gifting's finished." Johnna heard the kitchen door close and wondered what surprise could involve not only Luke and her mother, but the reclusive Calliope also.

Chapter 25

The doorbell rang, just as Charlie entered the living area in his new "Wild Things" pajamas. Answering the door, Lily said, "Hello. Please come in. Thank you for coming." She escorted Charles and Lisa Adcock and their petite, auburn-haired daughter into the foyer and called, "Charlie, your friend Amy is here."

Charlie came running and took Amy's hand. "Come see," he ordered, pulling Amy toward the dining table and leaving the adults to laugh at their abandonment.

"Please make yourselves comfortable," Lily said, directing them toward the living room seating. The bell rang again, and she returned to the door to greet Steve Daniels and his son, Alex. "Oh, Steve, how good to see you. And Alex, thank you for coming to Charlie's party." Alex, as blonde as his dad was dark, was obviously shy in the new environment and gripped his father's hand.

"Son, go play with the other children." Alex drew back, but his father insisted: "Alex, go on. I'm not leaving. I'll be here with the other parents."

Lily offered Alex her hand. "Let me show you what the children are doing. Your dad can go sit with the adults." Steve mouthed a silent, "Thank you," while Lily took Alex to have claws, horns, and tail attached. Lily was relieved when the child brightened with a giggle, as Charlie wiggled his backside in front of Alex and said, "See my tail."

When Johnna and Jess finished costuming their

small guests and left them to watch the animated Wild Things story, Lily brought her daughter and granddaughter into the living area to meet the parents. Lily said, "Charles and Lisa, Steve, these are my daughter, Johnna McGregor and my granddaughter, Jess." Turning to Johnna and Jess, Lily said, "Charles and Lisa are Amy's parents, and Steve is Alex's father."

"So pleased to meet you and thank you for coming" Johnna replied. After a polite exchange of words, she announced: "This is Charlie's first birthday party, and I appreciate your making it special for him. Now, if you will excuse us, we have a wild rumpus to oversee. Then, you can join us for birthday cake and ice cream. We're saving gifts for the last thing, because then we expect to lose control."

Lily joined the laughter, as she sat in one of the matching armchairs in front of the fireplace, opposite Steve Daniels in the other. "Steve, I'm so pleased you got Alex to come to the party. How is he adjusting? Is there anything more I can do to help? You know I'm always available for a hot meal and a good talk."

Lisa Adcock added, "Yes, Steve, we want to help, but we don't want to intrude."

Steve responded, "You ladies have been so gracious and thoughtful. So many in the church have helped us through terrible, dark days ... Angie's illness ... then her death. Alex still doesn't understand what has happened, why Mommy is gone. He understood her being sick ... he still could see her, feel her arms around him. But then, she was just gone. It will take time and maturity."

"Well, I'm sorry to have introduced sadness into the conversation, but I knew we'd have an opportunity to get you aside for an update and to offer our continued help. Of course, we are always praying for you and Alex," Lily assured him.

"Thank you," he replied. "That means so much."

Lily lightened the tone with the announcement, "I believe the wild rumpus has begun, which means cake and ice cream are close behind. I'll get the ice cream from the freezer and start scooping."

Chapter 26

Jess put the last package on the table, saying, "This one is from Mama and me." Charlie tore into the wrapping with enthusiasm. Upon uncovering the treasure, he clapped his hands, bounced with excitement, and shouted, "Wild things people! Wild things people!" Jess had known the figures of Max and the wild thing would be the perfect gift for Charlie, and Johnna had to agree. Though pricey, the creatures would give Charlie hours of contented, imaginative play.

Johnna began, "Well, Charlie, that seems to be the last ..."

"No, no, one more," Lily called from the kitchen. Coming into the dining room, she directed, "Charlie, stand over here, please. Everyone, gather around." Lily knelt in front of Charlie and said, "Charlie, close your eyes, shut tight. Don't open them." Addressing their audience, Lily said, "My friend, Calliope Winchester, has brought Charlie a birthday gift she has been keeping for me. A chorus of "Ohs" and "Oh, looks" greeted Calliope, as she entered from the kitchen. Setting the pup in front of Charlie, Lily said, "Open your eyes, Charlie. Meet another Max."

Charlie opened his eyes and cried, "A little Fwitz! Jess, Mama, a little Fwitz!" Charlie wrapped his arms around the puppy, now wriggling with excitement in the child's arms.

Getting his attention, Lily said, "Charlie, he will be

a smart dog, just like Fritz. And we will train him to protect you, just like Fritz did. But he will be your dog, to love and to grow up with you."

Jess could not restrain the tears that flowed when Charlie threw his arms around Lily's neck and said, "Thank you, Grandma. Thank you."

Wiping tears from her face, Lily looked up and said to those around her: "Charlie, Jess, Johnna, guests, we're not finished yet. Mr. Luke has a gift for Charlie also." Addressing Charlie again, she said, "Charlie, it takes time and hard work to train a dog to be like Fritz. We need all the help we can get. Mr. Luke has brought someone who can help Max to be just like Fritz."

Tears flowed from every eye when Luke entered from the kitchen with Fritz at his side—thin, limping, yet alive and whole.

Fritz sat at Lily's hand signal and allowed Charlie to cover him with kisses, as the child pressed his face into the dog's neck and cried, "Fwitz! Fwitz! I love you, Fwitz!"

"Charles, Lisa, Steve, do you mind if Jess takes the children outside to play with the puppy?" Lily asked the parents, who had returned to their seats in the living area.

Steve stood and replied, "I'll go with her. They might be more than a handful for one person." Lily knew Steve would not be comfortable with Alex out of his sight, and Jess would enjoy the outing more without the sole responsibility of supervision.

"Charlie, you, Amy, and Alex can take Max outside to play. Alex's daddy is going to help Jess watch you. Don't go near the road, and be gentle with Max." To Jess, Lily advised, "Keep an eye on the children, Jess, and don't let them get rough with the pup."

Charlie asked, "Fwitz come too?"

"No, Charlie, Fritz is going to rest on his bed a while. Take good care of Max."

"I will. Max my friend. I love him, Grandma." Lily was convinced the decision to introduce a new puppy was the right one. Though Fritz's ultimate outcome was uncertain at the time, she had thought a new puppy would be an emotional safeguard for Charlie and would allow Fritz a quieter period of rehab. Also, she was feeling the need to be challenged, once again, to train another fine animal like Fritz—and Max came from the same intelligent breeding stock of Wagner Kennels.

Chapter 27

Rocking in time to the melody she hummed, Calliope sat alone on the porch and watched cloud shadows playing on the mountain before her. Her memories were so real, she could almost sense Jeff sitting in the nearby chair. After one of Lily's delicious Sunday dinners, they would sit on the porch with coffee and plan the course of their future. Jeff said they would marry in the coming spring—here on the porch of Jeff's family home. Just closest family and friends would gather, as they spoke their vows under a bent willow archway adorned with spring flowers. Callie would wear a modest, ankle-length white lace dress with her favorite strappy sandals and carry a simple bouquet of violets. They would shop for Jeff's wedding attire, but it would consist of Levi's, plaid shirt, and sport coat. Lily would cater the reception in her home, from which they would leave to honeymoon at an "undisclosed location"—the cabin they had waited for months to share.

Then, Jeff would pass his boards and intern with a well-respected architectural group, while Callie taught at the college. They would save like crazy, so that Jeff could launch his own firm, where his unique talent and excellence would be the recognizable hallmark of every design. Their "alpha and omega" cabin might need some remodeling and additional space when children came, but that is where their life together would begin and where …

The front door opened, and a burst of three small children and an energetic puppy interrupted Calliope's reverie, followed by Jess, who nodded at her with a questioning expression. *You never know where I might turn up*, Calliope thought—and she might have surprised Jess by appearing in the white peasant blouse and long red floral skirt that had been Jeff's favorites.

"Excuse me, do you mind if I sit in this rocker?" asked the man trailing behind the children. Calliope recognized him as one of the parents.

"No ... no ... it's not taken." The man would never understand Jeff's presence had been there for half an hour.

The man introduced himself. "I'm Steve Daniels. That's my son Alex, the little blond fellow out there. You're Mrs. Craig's friend, Calliope. What an interesting name."

"I try to live up to it," Calliope responded.

"Quite a task: Calliope, the goddess of poetry and music, gifting artists with eloquence by touching their infant lips with honey."

Responding to her questioning expression, Steve Daniels said, "Excuse me. It's just a penchant I have for history, ancient religions—that sort of thing."

They rocked in silence. Calliope wished she could bring Jeff back to the seat this Daniels fellow now occupied. Though polite and cordial, he made her uncomfortable. She wanted to return to her memories, where reigned peace, love, and the sheer joy of being alive. Only cruel death had terminated the beauty of her world then, freezing its perfection in her mind, where she guarded it, keeping it safe and pure and allowing no one, nothing to intrude.

"I don't believe you were with Lily and the family this morning in worship. Do you attend?"

Calliope resented this stranger's presumptuous intrusion into her privacy. She smirked, "I wandered lonely as a cloud."

With a gentle smile, he replied, "Yes, but even Wordsworth said, 'When all at once I saw a crowd, a host, of golden daffodils.' He laughed, "I rather like thinking of us as daffodils."

Calliope stood and declared, "I must go," and she proceeded up the slope, past the mini barn, to a path that would intersect with one leading to the cabin. Again, she had ventured into the old world, where Jeff no longer existed, where thoughts and feelings were uncontrolled, disembodied spirits, who haunted, hurt, and confused. Her peace and security were in words, in books, in the nature with which she surrounded herself. This man had usurped her words to cast doubt on the validity of her chosen existence—a life without Jeff, but with memories of what was and visions of what might have been.

Chapter 28

With her sack of "goodies" in hand, Amy and her parents again expressed to Lily, Johnna, and Jess, their appreciation for the invitation and wished Charlie another "Happy Birthday," before exiting the front door. Steve Daniels lingered behind as Charlie and Alex finished their play, Jess gathered Alex's party favors, and Luke and Johnna circulated between kitchen and dining room, cleaning up the aftermath of rumpus. A tired puppy, Max, in his crate, had joined Fritz in Lily's bedroom.

Steve took Lily's hand and said, "Lily, thank you so much for the invitation. It has done Alex a world of good to be with the children, just to have fun. I think we both needed a wild rumpus," he laughed.

"It has been a good afternoon for all of us. Thank you for making the trip out here."

He hesitated, then added: "I'm afraid I may have offended your friend, Calliope."

"Calliope? When? ... How could you have offended her?"

"She was sitting on the porch when I went out with the children. I asked if I could sit in the other rocker, and she was okay with that. But, when I tried to make conversation, she suddenly said she had to go and beat a hasty retreat over the hill."

Lily replied, "I'm sorry, Steve. I'm sure you said nothing to offend her. Calliope's rather reclusive, not a people person or one to engage in small talk. Completely unlike her brother, Luke."

"Well, I hope you're right. She's an intriguing character, a child of nature and a poetic soul," he smiled.

"She thinks she's fiercely independent, Steve. But really, she's a sad, lonely woman, whose hope and joy are trapped in a world that ended nearly twelve years ago, when my son died. She and Jeff were to be married the spring after the accident, and she's never been able to move on with her life."

"I know how difficult that is—and how easy it would be to hang on to all that was Angie, to everything she touched, and never let go. But I have my work— reaching, teaching, and helping souls … and I have Alex, who needs to learn life goes on in this world, so that life can go on in the next."

Lowering her voice, Lily said, "Steve, when Johnna and Jess arrived, I thought you might be just the one to help them unshackle from the grief that has weighed on them since J. B.'s death." She paused. "I think being here already is helping them progress. But should you be looking for a real challenge, look no further than Calliope. Beneath that cantankerous, misanthropic persona lies a rich, deep soul, capable, obviously, of enduring love."

"Well, I'll keep that in mind. I'll have to decide if I'm up to what appears to be a uniquely stiff challenge." Turning toward the boys, he announced: "Alex, it's time to get back."

"But I want to stay," Alex argued.

Lily interjected, "Alex, you can come back when you have more time to play with Charlie. Your daddy and I will plan another get-together."

"Thanks, Lily. That would be much appreciated," Steve said as he scooted Alex out the door.

Closing the door behind them, Lily thought, *Steve*

Daniels may bring a whole new dynamic to this family—in more ways than one.

"Charlie's playing with his wild things, and I think Jess has retreated to her bedroom," Lily said, as she entered the kitchen to find Johnna washing and Luke drying dishes. "She's earned some quiet time alone."

"Thanks, again, Mom—for everything," Johnna said. "The party was exactly as I had hoped, and the surprises you and Luke and Calliope had—for all of us, were so special." Lily sensed her daughter's voice was quivering. "Max is a precious little puppy and ..." Johnna sobbed and dabbed her eyes with her forearm. "I can't even think about Fritz without getting teary." Luke put his hand on Johnna's shoulder and offered her the corner of his dish towel. Johnna laughed and said, "Thanks. Ranger Luke to the rescue, once again."

"That's our motto," he replied: "'Caring for the land and serving people,' including emotional women."

"Well, I'm not usually emotional," she defended herself.

"That's okay," Luke retorted, "I'm not usually that caring."

"I don't believe that for a second," Johnna replied, drying her hands on the proffered towel. She quipped, "I'm beginning to understand why mother doesn't mind feeding you to keep you around."

He shook his head in agreement. "I've warned her: 'Feed the Ranger, not the bears.'"

Lily observed their banter with new insight into the possibility surfacing before her. Luke and her daughter were developing a rapport—easy and comfortable. She wondered if they would realize what might be happening and, if so, whose eyes would be the first opened.

Chapter 29

Jess lay on her bed and tried to grasp her thoughts and understand her feelings about the events of the weekend. She had been so busy with preparations for the party, then with the festivities and interacting with the children, her mind was whirling. Only a couple of weeks ago, anger, grief, and resentment bound her in a small, predictable world, where her father was an amorphous monarch and her mother, an unappreciated regent in his stead. In the last few days, she had lived and was comfortable in the present. Now, she felt guilty that, during those days, California and what was left behind had no place in her mind—but worse, she had thought very little about her dad.

Jess remembered what Calliope had said: *"Write your thoughts and feelings on a page. Words ... make them real. ... They may give understanding of yourself ... "* Jess took a pen from the holder on the desk, plopped back down on the bed, and withdrew the red journal from the drawer of the bedside table. On the first page of the journal, she wrote: "Journal of Jessica Craig McGregor." She smiled to herself: *At least I remember my name.* Then, she turned to the next page and wrote: "Today was Charlie's "Wild Things" birthday party. Besides mother, Grandma Craig, and me, Luke was there and Charlie's friends, Amy and Alex, with their parents. Even Calliope came, to bring the new puppy she had been keeping for Grandma's surprise." Jess thought, *Those are the facts. ... Now, what about feelings?*

Charlie had a great time with his friends, though she observed Alex had a harder time getting into the fun and would run to his dad with the slightest of complaints. Jess knew his mother had died after months of cancer treatment. She could sympathize with his grief, but only imagine what it must be like for him, at the age of three, to lose his mother. Charlie had been too young to understand Dad was gone, while Jess had been old enough to become angry and embittered by his leaving. As Jess put her thoughts into words, she realized she had written, "I was angry because Dad left us." *Wait—what was that?* She read what she had written and then, read it again: *"I was angry because Dad left us."* How could such a simple statement startle and shake her? *I was angry. Why? Because Dad left us! We didn't leave him—Mother was the same mother, Charlie just a baby, and I was a sixth-grade girl with excellent grades and close friends. The only change in our family, in our life, was "Dad left us."*

Jess realized she had been full of negative feelings looking for a cause, someone to blame—her perfect, hero father, surely, would not be the source of her misery. But then, really, he had no intention of change or disruption on that final day. He was a test pilot who knew the risks and simply ran out of luck, as he might have said. Only her dad had taken any chances that day. No one, including her dad, had wanted anything to change—but he ventured outside the bounds and changed everything.

Now, she realized that, like Jess herself, her mother was trying to find a place in a world without J. B. McGregor. So, Johnna had returned to the place of her youth, where there was a loving mother, familiar surroundings, and memories of happy times—where there was uwohali. She smiled at the thought of the bird, living its long years in the valley. Her father had admired him and, she surmised, felt a sort of kinship with him. She determined she would get up early and go find him feeding...take her phone and try to get a picture...and her journal. Maybe there was something to what Calliope had said about words. If Jess had come to understand anything, it was she'd better try to adjust to life where she was—she was sure there would be no going back.

The chill mornings of spring were giving way to the humidity and promised sweltering of summer days. Having grabbed her backpack and chugging a glass of orange juice, Jess left her mother and Grandma Craig, still in their housecoats, rocking on the front porch as they cradled their coffee cups. Fritz, with Max lying close beside him, rested at her grandmother's feet.

"Be careful, Jess," her mother advised. "Watch out for critters."

"Yes," Lily agreed with a grin. "Four-legged, two-legged, or belly crawlers."

Jess laughed. "I will. I have my phone." Starting down the hill to the road, she called back, "I think I'll go down through the lower field to the river and walk along the bank."

Johnna called, "Be back in time for an early lunch. We have a few errands in town, and we'll check out the school."

Jess thought, *Well, that confirms we're here to stay.* Now, she wondered if "here" would be with Grandma Craig, or if her mother would choose to locate closer to the schools and conveniences of the suburb.

Chapter 30

Calliope had been up since dawn, even before uwohali made his first foray into the river. Perched on the largest rock of what she called "the tumble," she waited for the eagle's screech to signal the start of their new day. Only a few hours earlier, she was awake when Luke came home and tried to make his way silently up the stairs to the loft. Since the report of a second intrusion into a new-build down the road, he had made it his nightly mission to patrol the river road from the cut-off, past the cabin, down to the point the new settlement began. Not wanting to be suspected of nefarious intent by those who didn't know him, he'd do what he could to protect those who did, and to report anyone or anything questionable passing through their stretch of territory. The river road skirted the edge of the county, over the mountain, in the farthest reach of enforcement by the sheriff and his deputies. The newcomers had their handsome riverside treasure boxes in the beauty of nature, but they had given little thought to being "easy touches" in their seclusion.

Calliope loved her brother and appreciated his spirit of care and compassion. And she knew his love for her—and for Jeff, had brought him back home. She felt safe not only because of her brother's presence, but because Jeff had made the cabin her "port in the storm," a harbor from which she only set sail to replenish the necessities of life. Even her work allowed her the convenience of living in her head, of remaining secure in a fortress buttressed by words.

"Alpha and omega," Jeff had described the cabin that was to be their marital home. In the exuberant joy of youth, they would begin their life together. They would experience all the blessings and challenges—and children, that life would bring. And, in the end, they would hold each other's hand until one's time expired. But what had Frost said … "Ends and beginnings—there are no such things. There are only middles"? She knew she was living in a "middle"—she and Jeff had never begun, and there was no end to her wishing they had.

Calliope turned toward the screech and watched the eagle swoop from the pine stand to dive into the water. This time atsadi, the fish, eluded his grasp.

"He'll have to try that again." Jess' voice was soft, yet clear in the stillness of the morning.

"I see uwohali got you out of bed this morning," Calliope stated.

"I thought you would be here," Jess said.

"I am most mornings," confirmed Calliope.

Another screech, and they watched the eagle plunge into the water, then ascend with an enormous "breakfast" in his talons.

Without an invitation, Jess maneuvered her footing over the tumble to join Calliope.

They sat in silence, until Jess laughed and said, "You want to talk?"

"Not especially," Calliope replied, with a rare smile.

"For a woman who surrounds herself with words, you don't have many to say," Jess observed.

"And you seem to be unusually free with yours

today," Calliope retorted.

Jess reached into her backpack and retrieved the journal. "You were right—when I see them, the words help me understand."

When Jess offered the journal to her, Calliope said, "No, the words are yours. Tell me what you understand."

Jess was deliberate and careful, as she said, "I have been angry—at times, I still am. But I understand now, my anger should not be directed at my mother, but at change, and no one can do anything about that—it just is. My dad did his job, mother did hers, and we kids were just who we were at the time. When Dad died … just disappeared, we were the same, but everything was different. I have been angry at change, while Mom has been trying to find a way for us through it. Does that make sense?"

Calliope considered Jess' words, then responded, "More than you know."

They watched as a barge, moving upstream, peeked its prow around the bend in the river at the foot of the opposite mountain. Jess broke the silence, remembering, "Charlie said he wanted to be a tugboat when he grew up."

"Hmm," Calliope replied, "An appropriate metaphor for life—a tugboat pushing loads of varying kinds and sizes, often required to go upstream against the current."

"We studied metaphors and similes in fourth grade," Jess said.

"What grade will you enter in August?" Calliope asked.

"Seventh. I skipped second." She quipped: "I'm not sure if they thought I was advanced or if the second-grade teachers had been warned off."

"Do you like school?" Calliope asked.

"Oh, sure. I love to learn. I'm not a STEM geek. I'm more into humanities, but I make good grades in math—it's easy, like working puzzles. Mom said, after lunch, we're going into town to run some errands and check out the school—I don't know which one."

"We're districted for schools that are fifteen miles away, over the mountain, and the transportation department won't send a bus. The nearest school is in the next county, only about five miles away, but they'll charge tuition since you're out-of-area."

"I wonder if Mother knows that?"

"Lily likely told her." Calliope stood and said, "Come to the cabin."

Jess brushed the seat of her pants and picked up her backpack. "Oh, I forgot to get a picture of the eagle."

"If he is in your soul, you don't need a picture," replied Calliope.

Jess had a ready retort, but she kept silent for fear of hurting Calliope and losing their tenuous, incipient camaraderie.

Chapter 31

The secretary was a sturdy, silver-streaked brunette, fortyish, stylish, though casual in her summer-duty attire of white shirt and jeans. She stood as Jess and Johnna entered the glass-walled reception area of the office. "Good afternoon, Mrs. McGregor," she greeted them. "I'm Anita Fields, and this must be Jess." Shaking their hands, she said, "I'm so pleased to show you around our new facility. Our community has grown significantly, and we had more children than we could accommodate comfortably in the old building. This school was completed and opened to students only last year."

Johnna replied, "It is a modern, spacious building, and the grounds are lovely. Did I notice a walking trail on the campus?"

"Yes, our property abuts the community park, so we have access to the trail and the exercise stations along it. Many of our teachers—and parents, make use of it early in the morning or after hours." She laughed, "I need to make more use of it than I do."

Mrs. Fields led them along hallways, up and down stairs, through the STEAM departments—science, technology and engineering labs, art classrooms, and the mathematics wing. "We have six hundred students enrolled, with twenty assigned to each homeroom and a ratio of sixteen students per classroom instructor." Passing the computer lab, the secretary said, "Our tech lab is state-of-the-art. But you'll note, only next door is our traditional

104

library, housing a wide selection of research volumes, classics, and teacher-recommended books touching on contemporary issues."

After touring the cafeteria, auditorium, gymnasium, and athletics offerings, Johnna had to admit the facilities were impressive, expansive, and inclusive. Jess would have access to many learning opportunities and a wealth of resources and high-tech equipment.

Yet, something made Johnna uncomfortable. Jess had thrived in the classical education program of the private school in California. An hour from their home, Jess was willing, even eager, to rise early to make the daily drive across the dusty desert. Part of a group of mothers who carpooled their children, Johnna only made the trip to the city on Monday mornings and Thursday afternoons. While there, she would include shopping and hair appointments and, after Charlie was born, exercising in the park with the baby in a jogging stroller. After J. B. died, the school personnel and parents were caring and supportive, accommodating the family's need for time and healing. They were proud to claim Jess not only as an exemplary student in their program but were sad when the family they had come to love and appreciate left for Tennessee.

Johnna wondered what Jess' thoughts were about the possibility of this new school. Her daughter had been quiet as she toured the facility, her expression unreadable—observing, examining, questionless. Johnna was eager to make a cordial departure, without commitment to Mrs. Fields, and to tell Jess, "This is just an option. We'll check out others." As time-consuming and occasionally inconvenient as their school travel in California might have been, Johnna realized she would miss that aspect of their family life—and the friends and positive influence that came with it. She had been so occupied dealing with an unsettled present and trying to stay afloat in an overwhelming, unknown future, she had not appreciated the scope of Jess' sacrifice of friends and schooling.

Chapter 32

Jess relaxed when they returned to the recently purchased silver SUV, where Johnna started the engine and turned on the AC, before stating: "I would ask you what your thoughts are, but first I want to tell you mine." She considered her words, then continued: "It's an impressive school, judging from what we've seen. But I'm uncomfortable. Maybe it's just so different from what we had in California—or maybe it's just because we don't know any students, parents, or faculty yet." She reached over to the passenger's side to place her hand on Jess' shoulder. "Whatever it is, I realize how difficult it has been for you to leave your school and friends in California."

Jess sighed, relieved by her mother's words. "Thanks, Mom." Jess gazed at the school's façade and landscaping. "It's a nice building, and Mrs. Fields was friendly and kind to spend so much time showing us around." Jess was sincerely trying to be positive, when she said, "Maybe everything will be good when I make new friends, but it will be different—so many kids, just in three grades. We had half that many in the whole elementary school in California."

Her mother replied, "Well, you know, we have other options—other schools we can check out. Not far from here, there's a private co-ed school that would be as convenient to Grandma's as this one."

Jess ventured to ask, "Does that mean we're going to stay at Grandma's?"

"How would you feel about that?" her mother replied.

"Well, if you don't mind the inconvenience—until I start driving, of course," she teased, "I think staying with Grandma would be good for all of us. Charlie is happy being with the dogs, and we'd be around to help Grandma when she's older. And I really love the valley—even being where I can run into Calliope. As odd as she is, she's interesting … and caring in her own way."

"Jess, you may have thought about it already, though I haven't said anything— Grandma's house and land will be mine when she dies, which, of course, I hope is a long, long time away. Then, someday, it will pass to you and Charlie. So, it is a family home, a place where we can settle and feel secure." She smiled, "Rattlesnakes notwithstanding."

Jess felt it was time to be open with her mother: "I told you Calliope said Dad loved the valley. He saw uwohali, the eagle. I like to think Dad thought of him as a kindred spirit. I feel closer to Dad here than I did in California—there was nothing left of him there."

Jess was surprised when Johnna took a tissue from her purse and dabbed her eyes. "Oh, Jess, I miss him so much." Jess moved closer to hug her mother and to allow their tears to flow in unison.

Johnna retrieved another tissue from her purse for Jess, who blotted her eyes and wiped her nose. "I'm sorry, Mom, I haven't been very nice since Dad died. I've been angry and unforgiving, and I've directed those bad feelings toward you. You weren't any more responsible for what happened than I was. And there was nothing to forgive—no one did anything wrong. We were just who we were and did what we were supposed to do. But Dad's death changed everything. I guess I thought, if we stayed in California, somehow things could be the way they were. That was crazy—without Dad, everything had to change. I know you've been trying to do what's best for us."

"Jess, it means the world to me to hear you say that."

"And, Mom, I think you're doing a great job. Dad would be proud of you."

Johnna pulled Jess close again, and they purged their pent-up souls with more tears.

After lingering moments, Johnna moved Jess away and said, "Well, I'm about dried out. How about you?"

"I think I'm finished for a while," Jess agreed with a chuckle.

"Okay, this is what we're going to do. First, we'll have an early lunch and then some therapeutic ice cream. Then, I'll give the private school a call and see if we can have a look-around while we're in town."

"That sounds like a plan. But what's 'therapeutic ice cream'?"

"Oh ... chocolate, chocolate-peanut butter ... occasionally, strawberry with chocolate syrup."

Laughing, Jess suggested: "Why don't we just skip lunch and go straight to therapy?"

"Sounds good to me," Johnna agreed. "I won't tell my mother, and you don't have to tell yours." With a grin, Johnna shook her finger at Jess and warned, "But this won't be happening again, Miss Jessica. This therapy is a one and done, got that?"

"Got it. But I think I need super intensive therapy—maybe a triple dip Neapolitan fudge sundae with brownie bits."

"Ooh, you know, that sounds totally decadent—and delicious. We'll make that a double," she declared, as she put the vehicle in gear and backed out of the parking space.

Jess thought, *I don't think I'll be coming to this school. I don't know where I'll be in the fall, but I don't think it will be here. It just doesn't feel right.*

Chapter 33

Lily was relieved that, after the incident with the rattlesnake, her daughter felt confident about her watching Charlie while she and Jess went to town. She knew the girls would be away most of the day, and she prayed their time together would bring joyful, relationship rebuilding opportunities.

"Grandma, where is Mommy?" Charlie said, as he entered the kitchen, dragging behind him his well-worn Thomas the Tank Engine blanket.

"Hey, sweetie. Your Mommy and Jess are out on the porch. Let's take you to the bathroom, and then you and Max can go out and see them." Lily dried her hands and moved to pick up her grandson, still groggy and rubbing his eyes after his long nap. He had played in the yard with Max until all six of their legs threatened to collapse. Lily had brought them inside, where she cleaned Charlie's hands and face and fed him a hearty lunch of beef stew and corn muffins. Max finished his food and water, and Lily let him out the back door, just long enough to relieve himself. She tucked Charlie into the guest room bed with his blanket, and before she could shut the blinds and close the door, she saw Max was on the bed snuggled close to his boy. While they napped, she and Fritz lounged in the living room, and she read the latest news on her tablet.

Lily realized she had fallen asleep when she was awakened by a light rap on the front door. Peeking through the window, she was surprised to see Calliope, folder in hand, wiping her feet on the door mat. Fritz had raised his head awaiting her signal, so she motioned for him to stay, then opened the door. "Good afternoon, Callie. Come in. What brings you over here?" Motioning toward an armchair, she said, "Have a seat."

Without a word in passing, Calliope reached down to pet Fritz before sitting across from Lily. Handing Lily the folder, she said, "This is for Johnna and Jess. It's information about a Talented Students Project the college is beginning this fall. If Jess is the student I think she is, she'd qualify, and I would give her my recommendation. That folder includes all the information, instructions, and application form."

"Why, thanks, Callie. That's very thoughtful of you. They're checking out at least one school today and, I pray, having some quality girl-time."

"There's not much to choose from near here—the public school that would see Jess just as additional government funding, or the private school, where Johnna would pay nearly thirty thousand a year for Jess to be snubbed by snobs."

"Well, you certainly make either of those options sound unattractive," Lily chuckled. "Snob-snubbing sounds really awful," she joked, without reaction from Calliope.

"The college's TSP is an on-campus program for seventh through twelfth grade students, who meet certain requirements, laid out in the material," she gestured toward the folder. "The program includes all the basic courses required for graduation and for college admission, but the student may track in his or her fields of special interest and ability. Also, each student will be tested and placed in his grade level course based on scores, not age.

Jess might test seventh grade in math but tenth grade in language arts. She might pass competency tests in some courses and finish graduation requirements early, then take AP courses or more electives, or just go on to college."

"That's interesting. Is it costly?"

"There are some fees involved, but mostly for materials and equipment. The teachers come from the college faculty, who make time in their schedules to teach one course and receive a salary supplement from grant money the school has received for the project. Each class will be small with one-on-one interaction with the instructor."

"This sounds very interesting ..."

The front door opened, and Lily heard Johnna say, "I think I may be sick ... how about you?"

"Same here," Jess moaned, "but worth every potential puke."

Lily was thrilled at the sound of their laughter, but admonished, "Girls, Charlie's still sleeping. Come tell us about your fact-finding mission. Callie's here and has some more information for you."

Johnna and Jess lowered their voices. Johnna moved to sit in the armchair facing Calliope, and Jess sat next to her grandmother on the couch. Lily gave Jess the folder, which she perused while Calliope reviewed what she had told Lily.

"Wow, this sounds like a great program, but I'm not sure I'd qualify. I mean, I love school and learning, but I couldn't compete with the kids who'd be in this program."

Calliope answered: "That's the advantage of this program. Each student competes only with himself—each one's course is personalized. Grade reports consider only the individual student—if he or she has completed his assignments, mastered the material, and worked up to potential. When you finish or test out on courses required for graduation, you may take more electives or APs, or go ahead and enroll as a college freshman."

Johnna said, "Jess, this sounds like something you ought to pursue—a unique opportunity. But it is entirely yours to consider—your choice."

Jess closed the folder and replied, "I think I'll give it a try. What's to lose, except a little time and a lot of pride?"

Johnna said, "Thank you, Calliope, for telling us about this—and for offering to recommend Jess."

"My recommendation won't mean anything if Jess doesn't qualify otherwise. But I will do what I can." Calliope stood to leave and addressed Lily: "I never thanked you for the food you sent, back weeks ago. I appreciate your consideration. It was good, but for breakfast the next morning, Luke ate the leftovers I was saving."

"Well, he's likely to show up here this evening. How about staying for supper?"

"No, I need to get back. I have work."

Lily declared, "Well, I'll be sending him home with enough food for both of you and will order him not to eat your leftovers. But, please, we would like you to join us for dinner anytime. You have a standing invitation."

"Thanks" was Calliope's terse reply, as she let herself out the door.

Jess said, "I've never heard Calliope talk so much. She seems excited about this program."

"Yes. I don't know about you, Jess, but she sold me on it."

Lily said, "If you get Calliope talking about

something she's interested in, she is … what's the word? 'Loquacious'—not at all 'taciturn.' Johnna, you know we're going to have to start using big words around Jess, if she gets in this program."

Chapter 34

Lily was pleased and curious about the events of the day, as she, Charlie, and the dogs joined them on the porch. Johnna and Jess were rocking in unison, as Jess studied the TSP information and read parts aloud to her mother. Charlie immediately climbed into Johnna's lap, Jess picked up Max, and Lily and Fritz stationed themselves on the top porch step. "Well, we're all here now," Lily observed, "and I want to hear about your excursion into academia."

"More big words, Grandma?" Jess laughed. "Here, Grandma, take my seat," Jess offered as she stood.

"No, no," Lily declined, "I'm quite comfortable here, which tells me I need to cut back on the ice cream." Johnna and Jess looked at each other and giggled. Lily added, "I assume there's something you're not sharing with me."

Johnna said, "You assume correctly."

"Well, that's fine—Grandmothers don't need to know everything," she teased. "We're fragile."

"Yeah, right, Mom, that's the word for you," she laughed. She glanced at Jess and winked, before adding, "If your fragility can handle it—for lunch, we each had a triple scoop Neapolitan fudge sundae with brownie bits."

"Oh, no, you didn't!" Lily cried. "Without me? You stinkers!"

Charlie sat up on his mother's lap and grinned. "Mommy, Grandma said you stinkers." The women laughed, and Charlie repeated, "You stinkers!"

Johnna and Jess reviewed the events of the day with Lily, as Max and Charlie again played in the yard, with Fritz venturing out to be near them. The women were still enjoying their conversation, when Luke's truck pulled into the drive next to the SUV.

"Good afternoon, Luke," Lily greeted him.

As he made his way to the porch, Luke said to Charlie, "Come here, little man." Charlie ran to him, and Luke swung the child up on his shoulders and ran with him around the yard. Max nipped at Luke's heels and barked in defense of his boy, as Charlie squealed with joy. The experienced Fritz watched with interest, seeming to know the child was in safe hands.

Luke carried Charlie to the porch and set him in front of his mother. Charlie turned to take Luke's hand and cried, "Do again! Do again!"

Luke rubbed Charlie's head of dark curls and answered, "We'll go again in a little bit. Right now, go play with Max some more, while I talk to your mom, Ms. Lily, and Jess." Charlie jumped from the step to return to the dogs.

Lily continued, "You're here early, Luke. Who's minding the mountain?"

"I've got a sub for the afternoon. I had some other business. That's why I'm here. I wanted to give you all a heads-up."

Responding to the seriousness of Luke's expression, Johnna asked, "What's going on?"

"Well, most evenings, I've been kind of unofficially patrolling our stretch of road. There have been reports of break-ins in the new houses down the road—even one home invasion, though no one was injured, just terrified. I've been in contact with a deputy friend, who told me there has been a particular car described as being in the vicinity when the incidents occurred—the same one I've seen a couple of times."

"A fancy, dark, expensive looking one?" Jess asked.

"That's the way it's been described," Luke responded. "But I'm sure there's more than one of those down in the high-dollar area."

"Well, the one I saw, really close up, wasn't driven by a high-dollar looking person. He looked more like a gangster—dark, grungy, menacing."

Concerned, Lily questioned, "When was that, Jess?"

"When I was coming back from Calliope's after I went there to invite her to the birthday party. I got over to the side of the road as far as I could to keep from getting hit, and he looked at me like I was the one in the wrong place."

"Did you get a good look at him, Jess?" Luke asked.

"Oh, yes. I remember thinking I wouldn't forget his face, and I hoped he wouldn't remember mine."

Luke paused, before advising, "Don't any of you say anything to anybody about that. That may be helpful information, but best not to let it get outside the family."

"Right. Got it," Lily said, standing and brushing off her jeans. Jess, let's you and I go in and start dinner. It won't be long before we'll have to feed this ruddy ranger bear." As they entered the door, Lily continued, "There's you another word for your vocabulary—'ruddy.'"

"I've got that one, Grandma. King David was ruddy."

Luke sat in the rocker Jess had vacated. "So, we're

into vocabulary building now?"

Johnna informed Luke about Calliope's visit and the information she had given them. "I didn't know Calliope could be so talkative."

Luke responded, "Get her in her field of interest— her books, the college, she'll tell you more than you want to know." Luke said, "I think she's a bit of an Aspie, from what I've read."

"An Aspie?" Johnna questioned.

"Yes, on the autistic spectrum. She gets fixated on something, and she can't let go. She's outstanding in her field, but on a personal basis, she has difficulty with socialization ... interpersonal communication." He paused. "You know, I think that's why she can't let go of Jeff. She loved him and was comfortable with him. He was her world, and now, she can't leave that world. But professionally, she's amazing and well respected by the faculty. She has a tremendous knowledge of literature, authors ... she's practically a walking anthology of poets and poetry."

"That's interesting, but it seems she would be lonely. And she's such an attractive person, I'm sure she's had opportunities for dating, even marriage."

Luke laughed, "Not that she might have recognized. I'm sure her standoffishness and what can come across as rudeness has turned away some guys—and she sure wouldn't be one to flirt or give any indication of interest."

"That's rather sad," Johnna remarked.

"Really, not for Calliope, it seems. I think she's content with the status quo, where there is no fear of forming relationships and understanding their dynamics." They rocked in silence, before he added, "I'm glad I came back to keep an eye on her. She's independent but rather obtuse when it comes to reading people and their motives." As an aside, he said, "There's another vocabulary word for Jess."

Johnna laughed, "Yes, thank you. We will add that to her repertoire."

Luke continued: "Johnna, until this scoundrel or scoundrels are caught, be sure all the doors remain locked and you look to see who it is before allowing anyone in. I'll keep a check on you ... but I don't want anything to happen to any of you." Johnna was surprised when Luke reached to lay his hand on her arm. It was warm, heavy, and soothing in its muscularity. The gesture seemed so right, so easy, so normal, that all she could do was return a smile of pleasure and acceptance.

Chapter 35

"Let's serve the food off the stove and sit at the kitchen table," Lily suggested. "We can make room for the five of us. You can take up the mats and put the round cloth on the table. It's in the credenza."

On her way to the dining area, Jess passed by the front window and moved the blinds to check on Charlie and the dogs. She witnessed the gesture and response of affection between her mother and Luke, and she was overwhelmed by possibilities and scenarios she had never anticipated. *How could Mom even look at another man in that way? But ... why shouldn't she? She's still young. Luke is a nice person. He has shown he cares for us. I want to be angry ... I want to hide ... I want to understand.*

After allowing Jess time to complete the task, Lily followed her granddaughter, asking, "Jess, did you not find the tablecloth?" Appearing dejected and confused, Jess was standing at the window. Lily looked out and saw for herself the sight that was so disturbing. "Oh, I see," Lily said. She retrieved the tablecloth from the credenza and ordered, "Come on, Jess, back to work."

In silence, they continued preparation for dinner, until Lily asked, "Jess, did you ever think your mother might want a relationship with another man?"

"No, I guess not," she replied.

As she moved around the kitchen, Lily continued: "Did you know, statistics show that widows or widowers who have had happy marriages often long to have relationships like that again—and, if they marry again, those marriages are usually happy and durable? I think your mother may feel that way—she may miss the companionship and security of having a partner to share life's blessings ... and challenges. She and your dad loved each other very much. I know she wasn't always thrilled with military life, but she loved J. B. so much, she would have followed him to the ends of the earth."

Jess listened and tried to arrange her feelings into a folder of organized emotions.

"Luke is a very good man, Jess. He's not a dashing, heroic figure like your father. But he is loving, stable, loyal, and caring. There was someone he loved very much when he lived out west, but she wouldn't come with him back to Tennessee—she didn't love him enough. I want you and Charlie and your mother to be happy—and I want Luke to be happy. I hope you will give him a chance— give your mother a chance, if this is what it appears to be," she said, gesturing toward the porch. "Luke never could replace your father, but he could in a way be just who your father would want to take over his responsibilities."

Jess considered her grandmother's words and wondered: *What would Dad want ... for any of us? No man could be like dad ... could ever replace him, like Grandma said. But Dad would want us to be happy. especially Mom. He was never selfish ... he can't be now.* Her thoughts were interrupted by the door's opening and her mother's voice: "Charlie, come, let's get you washed up before dinner."

Lily said, "I was just about to call you all. Everything's ready." She pointed toward the annex and said, "Luke, get Fritz and Max settled down back there, please. I'll feed them after we eat. And you can use my bathroom to wash up."

Jess' mind whirled: *If Mom is going to date ... that sounds strange ... she couldn't do better than Luke. He's kind and handsome, in a rugged, ruddy kind of way.* She smiled at the appearance of the word again in her thoughts. *Grandma loves him ... he's already like family. This area is his home. We'd never have to move again.*

Johnna stationed Charlie in his booster, and Luke joined them, having put Max in his crate and Fritz on his bed in Lily's room. "Ms. Lily, you got some good smells going on in here again."

"Luke, I think you say that every time you start to sit at my table," she declared, flapping her dishcloth at him.

"And I mean it every time, too." Lifting pot lids, he investigated the offerings on Lily's stove. "Umm, green beans ... mashed potatoes ... oh, my favorite, fried apples ..." Peeking under the foil covering the casserole, he added, "And my favorite, baked crusted chicken."

"How many favorites do you have, Luke?" Johnna asked, laughing.

He answered, "Well, just about everything Ms. Lily fixes. She's always in my heart—I carry her memory wherever I go," he said, patting his belly.

Giggling, Lily ordered, "Hush up and sit down, Luke."

Their laughter brought them to tears when Charlie asked: "Grandma, Mr. Luke a stinker?" Seeing their amusement, he declared: "Mr. Luke is a stinker! Him a stinker!"

Jess giggled as she corrected him: "He is a stinker, Charlie."

"Uh-huh, he is a stinker!"

Chapter 36

After Sunday dinner, Jess rested on her bed and wrote in her journal. The past week had been strenuous—filling out papers, testing, and an interview for the TSP. She felt all had gone well, but there were twice as many candidates as there were spots available. If she wasn't accepted, she would have to go to the junior high they had toured—the private school was just too expensive. Insurance and the military's assistance for the families of those killed in duty had made ample provision for them, but the academy's tuition would eat through too much of their resources. Besides, Jess chuckled to herself, *I wouldn't want to be a victim of "snob-snubbing,"* as her grandmother had related Calliope's description of the environment.

As she recorded the events of the week and her hopes and feelings about her immediate future, a knock on the door and her mother's voice asking, "May I come in?" interrupted her concentration.

She closed the journal and tucked it away in the bedside drawer, responding, "Sure, Mom."

Johnna entered, sat on the edge of Jess' bed, and said, "I'm glad you've been able to rest this weekend. I know last week was nerve-wracking, but I can't help but believe you're a shoe-in."

"I hope so, but if not, I'll be okay. Don't worry, Mom."

"I won't. We'll make the best of whatever. And I

know you'll rise to the top, even if you must plow through five hundred ninety-nine ahead of you.

"That sounds rather bellicose," she laughed, reminding her mother of another new vocabulary word."

"Completely fortuitous on my part, rest assured," her mother retorted.

Johnna paused and then asked, "Jess, how are you feeling now ... about being here?"

"Copacetic, Mom. It's all copacetic."

"Okay," she laughed, "I mean really."

"Very acceptable, satisfactory, fine," she continued to tease.

Grinning, Johnna said, "Well, good ... really ... that's good to hear." Her mother seemed uncomfortable as she proceeded: "Jess, I'm hesitant to tell you, but before he left today after dinner, Luke asked me out on a date." Johnna lowered her head and shook it, saying, "That sounds so weird. I'm thirty-seven years old, and I'm asking my daughter if she thinks I should accept a date. Part of me feels like I'm seventeen again ... and another part like ... I'm betraying your father." Jess saw tears glistening in her mother's eyes.

"Mom, Dad's not here. You're still young—at least, not that old," she kidded. "Dad would want you to be happy—and safe, and who would fit the bill better than Luke ... a forest ranger?" She was happy to make her mother laugh, and she added, "Clean him up and put him in some 'fire' outfit, he'll likely be a 'babe magnet.'"

"A fire outfit? Why a fire outfit?"

"Oh, Mom, that just means 'trendy,' 'sharp.' You're so antiquated!"

"Jessica McGregor!" Johnna picked up the throw pillow near her hand and swatted her daughter, "You are a stinker!" She tickled Jess until she cried, "Enough! Okay, enough!"

Catching her breath, Johnna said, "Well, you haven't given me an answer. What should I tell Luke?"

"Where's he taking you?"

"He said something about dinner at a new restaurant in town, then a symphony pops concert at the river park."

"Ooh, posh ... the forest ranger has a classy streak. Do you want to go?"

"Oh, Jess ... yes ... and no ... I don't know. I'm nervous about it. I haven't been on a date since college, and then it was with your dad. I was young and in love. ... Then we got married, and I was happy and comfortable. ... I don't know. I'm comfortable now, with you kids and Grandma, but I think about the years ahead ... when all of you are gone ... I think I'd be lonely without a special someone in the other porch rocker," she smiled.

Jess thought, then declared: "Okay, let me tell you what to do. Say yes, but tell Luke, right up front, how you feel—just tell him what you've told me. He should be like a brother to you, from what Grandma says, so ... easy to talk to. Just go on the date, enjoy the food and the music, and just see where it goes from there—maybe just a good time between friends, or maybe ... 'moonlight and roses,' like that funny old song Grandma sings sometimes."

Johnna thought and concluded, "I guess you're right." Then she asked, "Help me decide what to wear? Maybe we could even go shopping—another girls' outing?"

"Sounds good, but we'd better pass on another fudge sundae," Jess advised. "Grandma would not be happy if we got ice cream again without her. And, really, you're at the age when you should start being careful about that middle-age muffin top."

"Why, you stinker!" Johnna picked up the pillow again and beat and tickled her daughter, until she screamed for mercy.

* * * * * * *

Having cleaned up the kitchen, Lily settled on the couch with her tablet and with Fritz by her side on the floor. Charlie was taking his nap with Max in the guest room, where they would not be disturbed by the commotion coming from Jess' bedroom. Lily was overjoyed to hear the happy, girly silliness coming from Johnna and Jess. She was thankful for the progress made in their relationship since Johnna had brought the children back to Tennessee.

Lily believed in God's blessings, beginning with the land, so touched by His creative artistry. She was thankful for her family, for her friends, and for more things than she could begin to count. She knew there would be challenges—they were as necessary as blessings, for growth and strength. But her family was together—and, together, they could face any difficult, uncertain future. *After all,* she thought, *the future is just a series of "todays" that can be full of love, support, and cooperation.* Lily leaned her head back on the couch; the tablet dropped to her lap; and the sound of her soft, Sunday afternoon snoring caused Fritz's ears to twitch.

Chapter 37

Calliope rocked under the overhanging roof of the porch, protected from the gentle early morning rain, now just a refreshing mistiness. The fog was beginning to dissipate—"billows of pillows of ethereal mist," as a poet once described the ground-hugging clouds. She loved the warmth of the sun on her face; but on mornings like this, when she was wrapped in her woolen comforter, she felt cozy, calm—at peace in the solitude of her existence, in the stillness of her mind. With her studies and teaching, her mind was comfortably full of knowledge she could access and control. With her memories of Jeff, it was filled with sweet sadness, cushioned by the sympathy of nature and her poet friends. When people entered her world of thought, with their emotions, judgments, opinions, and incessant mundane speaking, her mind was full of sparks igniting nothing but confusion.

She would go to the college today and, perhaps, get the results of the TSP selection. She wanted Jess to be accepted, but Calliope was not allowed to influence the decision; the sole determining factor was the candidate's performance on the battery of tests and the interview. Calliope liked Jess—she was not full of meaningless words, and she shared the kinship of uwohali. Calliope believed Jess had the intelligence and strength to absorb learning, to sift wheat from chaff, and to develop her abilities and discernment while maintaining a unique and independent spirit.

Calliope

If Jess was accepted into the program, she might ride with Calliope on her teaching days. Though she never knew her uncle, Jess reminded Calliope of Jeff—perhaps, it was some family resemblance, some mannerisms he and Johnna had shared that were passed to Jess, or simply that Jess and Jeff were not idly talkative—silence was not a void to be filled with unnecessary words. Calliope would be glad to have her accompanying her to the college; driving was necessary, but unpleasant for Calliope, who had obtained her driver's license and purchased the old Forester only shortly before she began teaching.

Calliope heard the hum of the engine turning at the lane before she glimpsed the shiny black sedan coming toward the cabin. The driver parked behind the Forester, picked up some papers, closed the door behind him, and made his way toward the porch. "Good early morning … Miss Winchester, I believe it is?"

Without responding, Calliope tried to comprehend the words that flashed in her mind: *"'Prophet!' said I, 'thing of evil!—prophet still, if bird or devil!'"*

"Well, assuming you are Miss Winchester, your neighbor said I might find your brother Luke here."

Neighbor? My only neighbor is Lily, she thought. How would she know this man? "My brother is not here," she told him.

He continued: "I am Leonard Emory. I deal in properties along the river. Please tell your brother I came by." He took a business card from the pocket of his blue shirt and wrote on its blank reverse side. Handing it to Calliope, he said, "Just give him this, please. He'll know who I am."

Calliope watched as the man returned to his car and backed down the lane to the road. She saw the card simply identified the man as "Leonard Emory." She turned it over to read his written message: "Now that I know where you and your sister live, I may be back."

It was still early; but knowing Lily to be an early-riser, Calliope put the business card in her pocket, pulled on her boots, took her hat from the doorway hook, and began the short trek across the hill. She found Lily, as Calliope herself had been—coffee in hand, rocking on the front porch. Fritz raised his head and swished his tail in recognition of a friend, as Calliope ascended the steps and sat in the accompanying rocker.

Chapter 38

"Good morning, Callie. What brings me the pleasure of your company this fine early morning? How about a cup of coffee?"

Without answering, Calliope handed Lily the card from her pocket. "Do you know this man? He knew my name. He said my neighbor told him where to find Luke. You are my only neighbor."

"Well, you have other neighbors, Callie," she smiled, "but I guess none you would count." Lily took the card. She felt a quickening of her pulse and a constriction in her chest, as she read both sides of the card, then inquired: "Callie, what did this man look like? What kind of car did he drive?"

Calliope appeared bewildered before replying, "He was dark. The car was dark. Words from Poe's 'The Raven' popped into my mind."

Without speaking, Lily pondered the best course of action, as Callie waited and petted Fritz—an action Lily knew to be as calming to Callie as to the dog. "What are your plans for today?" Lily asked.

"I must change clothes and be at the college by nine o'clock. I have a summer class at 10:15 at Hutchison Hall, then some preparation for the upcoming quarter, in my office in the Humanities building. I will be able to leave about 2:45 this afternoon."

Lily directed: "Callie, get ready for work and go to the school as soon as the doors open. I know you will want to put on something more comfortable after work. Take those clothes with you and come back here to change. Don't go to the cabin right away. You and Luke will eat dinner with us, and we'll talk about this man. I have not met him—I know nothing about him. I know he made you feel anxious, or you would not be here—the words would not have come to your mind. Trust the words, and do not trust that man."

Lily watched as her friend, a second daughter to her, made her way back over the hill and disappeared past the mini-barn. Pieces were coming together about Luke, the car, the man, and Jess' identification of him—and Lily was distressed at the puzzle picture forming in her mind. She knew Calliope to be an intelligent, independent woman, but not the greatest judge of character. She remembered Jeff's saying she was gullible and lacked the usual womanly intuition, but he loved her quirkiness and absence of guile and was determined to be her knight guardian. If only …

Lily remembered the cell phone she had slipped into the pocket of her robe. The service was not always reliable on the mountain, so she texted Luke: "Callie just left. Dark man/car at the cabin. Made Callie anxious. Left a note that seems menacing. She's coming here after school. Have supper with us if you can, so we can talk." She was glad when he got right back to her with a "thumbs up." She knew she would feel more secure with all her family sheltering in place this evening under her roof— and knowing Luke was authorized to carry a firearm.

Lily continued her morning ritual of rocking, when she usually contemplated the day's activities and counted her blessings with the reminder, "This is the day the Lord has made; We will rejoice and be glad in it." But today, her musings competed with Callie's intriguing information and the sinister message. She knew Callie understood things differently, but her grasp of the "darkness" of her morning visitor was revealing. Lily was relieved when Callie in "Old Blue," as she and Luke called her vehicle, passed the house on her way to the college. With everyone safely occupied, Lily would have the day to prepare not only dinner, but to garner all the information she could from neighbors about the activity of the suspicious man and his car. Jess and Johnna would be shopping in Chattanooga, this time taking little man with them for a special outing, and Callie would be ensconced in the amicable society of poets and authors. Lily would load Fritz and Max in his kennel into the Jeep, make a short run to the grocery store, and on the way, stop to check with neighbors, to get input and to give warning.

Chapter 39

Lily's Jeep was gone when Johnna and Jess returned for Charlie to take his nap. Johnna was thankful her mother and the dogs were still away, so she could get Charlie settled without distraction. His legs had tired early, so Johnna had rented one of the mall's strollers, a red fire engine, which Charlie steered and clanged for what seemed like miles, as she and Jess searched for the perfect "first date" outfit. They settled on a sleeveless, blue floral, A-line midi-dress, with a blue elbow-length shrug. Jess said the color was the perfect shade for her mom's eyes and accentuated her blondness. Also, Johnna's simple silver bangle bracelet and opal pendant earrings would be perfect accessories, with her beige strappy sandals and straw clutch. Jess declared she should be "summer casual formal," though Johnna doubted such a style existed.

Johnna dropped her handbag on the couch, carried Charlie directly to the guestroom, and tucked him into his youth bed. He was too tired to notice Max was not next to him in his kennel.

"Mother!" Jess screamed, "Mother, come quick!"

Closing the guestroom door behind her, Johnna rushed to find Jess standing in her bedroom. All the drawers were open, the pink jewelry box was gone from the dresser top, and the red journal was lying open on the bed with words scrawled across two pages: "I MAY BE BACK."

"Jess, don't touch anything. I'll get my phone and

call 9-1-1." Retrieving the phone from her bag, Johnna said, "Let's check the annex." While waiting for the call to connect, they moved into Lily's office, where, again, drawers were open—then, into the bedroom, where on the mirror were words that appeared in the shade of Lily's lipstick: "POOR DOG, DEAD DOG." The exterior annex door was standing open.

The sheriff's dispatcher said a deputy would be there within half an hour. Johnna returned to the guestroom, picked up her sleeping child, and she and the children moved to the front porch to await help, whenever it might come.

They heard the siren long before the patrol car appeared. The deputy pulled off-road, well up into the yard, and Luke's truck was right behind him. As the deputy finished a call on his radio, Luke ran up to the porch and knelt in front of Johnna and Jess, asking, "Are you alright?"

Johnna answered, "We're both shaken, but okay. Charlie has slept through everything. ... I don't know what was taken, other than my old jewelry box, though I haven't checked. Mainly it seems to have been a warning. ... I think you need to see inside."

Luke gripped Johnna's hand and caressed Jess' cheek as he moved to follow the deputy into the house. Johnna noticed Luke was wearing his holstered pistol, and she wondered if had left the station in a hurry and forgot to leave it in the truck, or if he thought he might have need of it.

Luke and the deputy were still in the house when Lily pulled into the driveway and parked beside Johnna's SUV. With Fritz following, she sprang from the Jeep and raced to the porch asking, "What's wrong? What's happened? Luke was on the annex porch and waved me around to the driveway."

"Grandma, here, sit down," Jess advised, as she moved to sit on the porch step.

Johnna reviewed what had transpired, and Lily was alarmed and perturbed that their home, their haven of peace and security, would be so cruelly violated. "Why would anyone be so malicious ... so inhumane?"

Johnna replied: "This may be the same guy or gang that have moved up-river from their criminal activity in the new-builds. Maybe they didn't find anything they considered of value to steal, but to me it looks more like a warning."

Lily said, "I was saving this to give to Luke." Handing the business card to Johnna, Lily added, "This is the second warning today, almost surely from the same man. He was at the cabin early this morning and left this card with Calliope to give to Luke. She was concerned enough that she immediately came to me. The man told her a neighbor, whom she assumed to be me, had told him where to find Luke. I think this fellow knows Luke has been on the lookout for him—he may know Luke's part of the County Community Patrol. I told you Luke trained out West as a Wilderness First Responder, but he worked in forest law enforcement. He could be a particular threat to these two-bit criminals."

"But," Johnna observed, returning the card to Lily, "it seems they have gone from break-ins and burglaries to home invasion. I'm sure that escalates the degree of the crimes."

Luke and the deputy exited the front door. "We locked the annex door, Lily. This is my friend, Deputy Jack Collins. He called me on his way over the mountain to tell me about the reported break-in here."

Lily and Johnna nodded, and the deputy said,

"Pleased to meet you. Sorry it was like this."

"There doesn't seem to be any damage," Luke reported, "but you'll have to check to see if any valuables are missing and include them in the report."

"Ladies, if you will come with me back into the house, I need to fingerprint you three, just to exclude your prints from ones we have lifted, though I'm guessing the perpetrators wore gloves."

Charlie was beginning to stir, waking up from his nap. "Mommy?" he whimpered.

"Charlie, Mr. Luke is here. He's going to stay with you for a few minutes."

Johnna handed the child to Luke, as Lily cried, "Oh, me, I've got to get Max out of the Jeep. He and Fritz both need water by now."

Max wriggled to be released, saying, "I get down, Mr. Luke. See Max." Luke freed the child and watched as boy and dog were reunited.

As the deputy printed each woman, the others checked their jewelry, money, or electronics and found nothing missing except the pink jewelry box. The deputy said the felon likely wanted to get in and out in a hurry and seized the opportunity for an easy grab of something that might contain valuables.

"It contained nothing much, really, except a silver charm bracelet worth a lot of memories," Johnna declared. "But you called him a felon." As she cleaned her fingers with the wipe he provided, she asked: "Is that because of the home invasion down the road?"

"Yes, ma'am, that's aggravated burglary, a Class C felony," the deputy responded. "When we get this guy and his gang, they'll have some heavy time to pay."

The deputy packed his print kit, made more notes on the form, and had Lily and Johnna sign the report.

Standing to leave, he said, "I'm sorry about this, ladies. Just keep your doors locked. Luke can advise you on other precautions and safeguards—and likely get here faster than I can in case of emergency. If there is any other problem, call 9-1-1, then call Luke."

"Oh, Mom," Johnna remembered, "give the deputy that business card."

"Deputy Collins, I believe the same man who did this showed up at Calliope's cabin this morning and told her to give this to Luke."

Jack Collins looked at the card front and back and passed it to Luke, who, frowning, read it and returned it to Collins for him to clip to the report. "This may be helpful, though 'Leonard Emory' is surely an alias."

When Collins left in the patrol car, Johnna and Jess immediately started righting things inside, returning drawers and cleaning the mirror, so that nothing was visibly amiss. Lily and Luke moved their vehicles to their usual annex side parking. As Calliope's "Old Blue" pulled into the driveway beside Johnna's SUV, Johnna and Lily were sitting in the rockers, watching as Jess and Luke played with Charlie and the dogs in the front yard. Fritz, now stronger and eager to join the fun, stood on alert near Max and was ready to chase any errant tennis ball. They all wanted things to seem normal for Charlie and, when Calliope arrived, to give her an account of the events in a calm and comfortable setting.

With a backpack slung over her shoulder, Calliope approached the steps. Lily greeted her: "Good afternoon, Callie. How was your day."

Calliope responded: "'My spirit, like my spine, ardently prays for rest."

Johnna chuckled at Lily's amused response:

"Callie, dear, why can't you just say, 'I'm tired'?" With obvious affection, Lily continued, "Come up here and let me talk to you." Johnna moved to sit on the porch step, while Callie sat in the rocker and Lily related to her the events of the afternoon.

Luke left the children and joined the women. Rising from her rocker, Lily said, "Here, Luke, take my seat. I'm going to start supper. I've explained to Callie what happened this afternoon. You carry on and fill me in later."

Johnna was impressed by the kind and gentle manner with which Luke dealt with Calliope, reassuring her and easing her anxiety. At the same time, he was returning to Johnna a sense of security—a confidence that she could have control over their circumstances. She listened as he laid out simple procedures: always locked doors, cell phones at hand with emergency numbers on speed dial, windows closed and latched, and in every room, access to something that could function as a weapon, like a fire poker, rolling pin, or ball bat. He said those precautions should be standard, under any circumstances, particularly when women and children were on their own. Johnna was surprised—and concerned, when Luke's final directive was for Calliope to return to the cabin after supper and to follow his directions—that all would be safe for her there, and for everything at Lily's to return to the status quo, after taking the safeguards he had outlined. He said, "I plan to have the problem remedied, hopefully before this night is over."

Johnna was giving Charlie his bath, and Jess and Calliope were sitting on the front porch, while Luke and Lily remained at the kitchen table with their after-supper coffee. With lowered voice, Luke asked, "Ms. Lily, are you still young and fit enough for a little adventuring?"

"Luke Ferguson, how dare you even ask! What have you got in mind?"

Chapter 40

The evening seemed as tranquil as the day had been tumultuous. In the gathering dusk, Jess and Calliope rocked in silence as they watched the flicker of lightning bugs and listened to the soothing hum of an outboard going upriver.

Jess flinched when Calliope unexpectedly spoke: "Orientation is in three weeks."

"What? What orientation?" Jess asked.

"You were accepted into the TSP. You passed all the tests, and they said you were mature and well-spoken in your interview."

"Well, Calliope, thanks for remembering to tell me—I might not have shown up." Jess tried not to sound testy in her response.

Calliope continued: "They'll send an official letter of acceptance. I was able to get the results early. It's a good program, interesting. You should do well. I can give you a summary of what's covered in each class. Seventh grade is a lot of review. You might test out of some classes."

Jess was thankful and excited but restrained by Calliope's impassive nature. "Thanks, Calliope. I am very appreciative of your help, for all you have done."

"I just gave you information," she responded. "You did this yourself—your industry and intelligence. Get through the requirements. Test out of what you can. Choose to study what you love: 'It is easy to work when the soul is at play' … Dickinson."

Jess thought about Calliope's unusual flow of words. A thought came to Jess: "Will you be teaching in the TSP?"

"Two classes, 'British Literature and Poetry' and 'Introduction to Shakespeare.'"

"Interesting. I look forward to being in your classes," Jess said.

"Only serious students have qualified for TSP. I like to teach a student who values learning, not a brainless body that wastes classroom space. Shakespeare said, 'He has not so much brain as ear-wax.'"

Jess laughed at Calliope's reiteration of Shakespeare's indelicate description and returned to rocking and considering the situation at hand. She asked, "Are you going back to the cabin this evening?"

"Yes, Luke says it's safe. I'll follow his precautions."

In a moment, Luke came out on the porch, handed Calliope her backpack, and said, "Callie, let me follow you to the cabin. I'll get you settled and make sure everything is secure." Calliope made her way down the steps as Luke continued, "Wait for me. I'll get the truck and be right behind you."

Jess called after her, "Calliope, thank you for telling me about the TSP. Be safe."

"I will," she replied. "'Sleep! Sleep safe till tomorrow.'"

Jess asked, "Shakespeare?"

"Williams," Calliope called back.

Jess watched as Calliope backed out of the drive and waited on the side of the road until Luke's truck was behind her, and together they proceeded toward the cabin.

Jess' mind was filled with thoughts of the day, as

she entered the house, locking the front door behind her and sliding into place the high, child-proof latch her mother had installed. She proceeded through the annex to the exterior door to ensure it also was locked and latched. She found her mother and grandmother in the kitchen at the kitchen table. "The front door and annex door are secured," Jess informed them.

Pointing to the kitchen access, Lily added, "So is this door—and all the windows are locked. But I don't think we have anything to be concerned about. We just got an ugly warning. Whoever our intruders were, they saw we don't have a lot of valuables they'd be able to fence."

"On a brighter note," Jess began, seating herself at the table, "Calliope told me I've been accepted into the Talented Students Program at the college."

"Oh, Jess, that's wonderful!" Johnna exclaimed, rising to hug her daughter.

Grasping Jess' hand, Lily added, "Oh, dear, that's the best news of the day!"

Johnna continued: "How do you feel about it?"

Jess paused. "I'm pleased—a bit nervous, but excited." She chuckled, reminding her mother of the recent scenario: "And I don't have to fight my way to the top through five hundred ninety-nine bodies. Orientation is in three weeks," she added.

Enthused, her mother suggested, "Let's go shopping for you—some new clothes and backpack, maybe a laptop or new tablet. And we'll find a good salon where we can get our hair and nails done."

"Mom ... this is not a beauty contest."

Lily gripped Jess' hand. "No, Jess, but this is the beautiful new beginning of an exciting stage of your life. We want to celebrate it and share it with you. And count on me to foot the bill on the laptop, tablet—any technological gadgets of your choosing."

"Oh, Grandma, thank you. That's so generous of you," Jess replied.

"Mom, thanks," Johnna agreed. "That's much appreciated."

"You're welcome," Lily responded, "but it's just my investment in posterity and in fodder for future bragging."

Jess stood and gave her grandmother, then her mother, a hug. "I think I'll go to my room and reconnoiter what I've got, see what still fits and what I might need."

Lily laughed, "I guess we'll be living in a world of big words for the next several years."

Johnna responded, "We'd better keep a Funk and Wagnalls on hand."

They laughed when Lily said, "Oh, Johnna, even I know that is so passé."

Chapter 41

When they heard Jess' bedroom door close, Lily said, "Johnna, I am so proud of you and Jess. It seems you finally have weathered the storm."

Johnna agreed: "We are in a good place right now. I credit you ... and Luke—even Calliope, with getting us to this point. Coming home was the only option I had left, but I am convinced now it was the right choice. You have given us a home and stability. Luke gives us a feeling of safety, even in this current situation. And Calliope ... well, in her own way, I think she has given Jess a grounding, kind of shoring up her emotions. ... I don't know exactly how to explain it. We can't pinpoint providence, but maybe it's simply providence, using each of us to supply a piece to put the puzzle together."

Lily constrained the emotion that threatened to overwhelm her, realizing she had to be controlled and thoughtful for the task ahead. She took her daughter's hand and said, "Johnna, dear, I love you all so very much."

"We love you too, Mom."

Lily sniffed and proceeded: "Changing the subject—Fritz and I are going on patrol with Luke tonight.

"Oh, Mom, no, that's not safe," Johnna argued.

"No, it's perfectly safe. We're just going to do our own reconnoitering," she smiled. "This morning I checked with a few neighbors who have seen the black car. One told me she saw it several times, parked behind the restaurant up on the highway. I want you to lock and latch the door behind me. I'll let Max out to do his thing before

I leave; then you settle him next to Charlie—you know Max's signals. He's ready to be free of his crate at night, and he'll recognize and bark at any unusual noise."

"Okay, got it. But, please, be careful—both of you."

"We will," she assured Johnna. "Oh, by the way, I got a couple of clubs from your father's old golf bag and put one next to Jess' bed and one next to yours. I don't think there'll be any need for them—just following Luke's orders."

Twilight had faded to darkness when Johnna and Max followed Lily and Fritz to the annex door. Luke's truck, engine running, was waiting in the drive next to Lily's Jeep. Lily gave Max the signal to stay and left Johnna to resecure the premises. Lily was thankful Fritz's strength was renewed to the point he was able to jump into the truck bed when she lowered the tailgate. Then, she climbed into the passenger side and said, "Lily and Fritz reporting for duty."

Luke responded, "Let's just hope we see some action."

As they drove up the road toward the highway, Lily noticed a shotgun in the rack behind their heads. Also, Luke had added a two-way radio to his belt. Though she couldn't see it, she assumed his nine-millimeter Smith and Wesson was still at his side.

Motioning around the cab, Lily asked, "I assume you are authorized to carry all this stuff, and I'm not going to be arrested as an accomplice for anything?"

"Check the glove box," he told her.

On top of his maintenance and insurance papers lay his ID and badge. Looking them over and raising her eyebrows, she said, "Well, I see," and returned them to the compartment. "I'm okay then. Let's go get 'em, Buford."

Turning into the crowded parking lot of the restaurant, Luke said, "We'll pull over under the trees near the river. We'll be shielded but can get a glimpse of the backdoor." As he turned off the engine, he said, "Well, would you look at that—our friend is here." Sarcastically, he added: "He's unloading stuff from the trunk of his shiny, black, expensive crime car."

Lily waited in anticipation, as Luke picked up his two-way and said, "Collins, Ferguson here. What's your location?"

"County line, your side of the mountain."

"Suspect vehicle located behind restaurant on the river, just outside your county. Have you notified the jurisdiction officers?"

"10-4, They're waiting our signal to approach."

"Give 'em the go-ahead." Turning to Lily, he said, "Get ready."

Feeling as if she was in an episode of Cops, Lily's pulse raced as she heard the siren approaching in the distance. Appointed back-up if needed, she took her position at the bed of the truck and lowered the tailgate. Fritz sat on alert.

They watched as the man, hearing the siren, slammed the trunk down and jumped behind the wheel of the sedan. Luke bounded from the truck and ran toward the car while drawing his weapon. Before the felon was able to back up and put the vehicle in drive, Luke appeared at the open car window and ordered him to turn off the engine and throw the ignition keys out on the ground.

The perp complied, then threw open the door and rammed it into Luke's thighs, causing him to lose his footing. The felon seized the opportunity to escape, running toward the river and the boat dock.

Lily shouted, "Fritz, attack!" and pointed toward the fleeing criminal. Fritz sprang from the truck, raced to the man, and had him in the clench of his powerful jaws, refusing to let him go as the man struggled and tried to bat Fritz away. When two police cars halted in the parking lot, the sirens stopped, and a pair of jurisdictional officers ran from their vehicle to take custody of the suspect, as Lily called the signal to "Halt!" Fritz sat and stood guard while the officers made their arrest, and Lily ran to see if Luke was injured.

"Are you alright?" she asked, as he was holstering his handgun.

"Well, my ego has suffered some bruising," he admitted with a grin.

As the officers loaded Emory, struggling against his restraints and shouting, "You haven't seen the last of me, Ferguson!" Jack Collins exited his deputy's car and sauntered over to where Luke and Lily stood. "Well ... old buddy ... looks like Granny and the dog collared your perp—no offense, ma'am," he grinned, tipping his hat to Lily.

"None taken," she laughed.

"Well, Mr. Funny Guy, I'd advise you to have the officers check out the kitchen staff of this restaurant. I'd wager you'll find some accomplices in there with a stash of stolen goods." Luke put his arm around Lily's shoulder and said, "Granny, let's get you home. It's past your bedtime."

"Fritz, come!" Lily called, pulling a treat from her jacket pocket. Fritz rushed to receive his reward, with hugs, pats, and loving words: "Here, my beautiful, strong, courageous boy—you are a hero once again." Fritz seemed to revel in the action and subsequent attention, but Lily knew he would welcome and deserve a sound night's rest. Lily knew that she, on the other hand, would have to let the excitement and adrenaline surge calm before she could even consider sleep.

As they walked toward the truck, they passed by the patrol car holding the so-called "Leonard Emory," who, from the window of his sealed enclosure, grimaced and spat at them.

Luke kidded, "And a very good evening to you, too, Mr. Emory."

Lily said, "I can hardly wait to get home and tell Johnna and Jess what happened."

"Ms. Lily, maybe you can leave out the part where I looked like a complete idiot."

"How about I just let you give the recap?"

"No, now … you can tell them."

"Ha! You know you'd have to be honest and tell them everything," she accused, poking him in the side. "Well, that means they get 'the whole truth and nothing but the truth,' or we just say, 'We caught the bad guy.' What's it going to be?"

"Okay … then … 'We caught the bad guy.'" Luke hugged her to his side and said, "I'm kidding, just kidding. Tell them I blew it, and Rin Tin saved the day."

Chapter 42

Johnna entered Jess' bedroom, where a chair waited before the dresser, and Jess stood behind it, ready to make adjustments to Johnna's date prep. "No, Mom, don't pull your hair back," Jess ordered. "Sit down." Taking the clip from her mother's hair, Jess said, "Just let it be loose. I'll smooth it with the flat iron and maybe just turn the ends under a bit."

Johnna was leery about Jess' coming toward her with a scorching hot device akin to a branding iron, but Jess had time and effort invested in this date—and she knew more than Johnna about current styles.

Assessing her mother in the mirror of the dresser, she said, "Your make-up looks good, maybe just a little less lipstick and a bit more gloss."

"Jess, I don't know about all this. Luke asked the ordinary, everyday Johnna for a date. He's going to know this isn't the natural me."

Jess huffed. "Mom, we're simply accentuating, not concealing ... well, not much ... just the dark circles a bit. And I've read that a man likes to be seen with a beautiful woman on his arm ... and, Mom, you are ... you know... gorgeous."

"Oh, Jess, thank you, sweetheart. I haven't heard that since your dad was alive."

"I know. I remember how he used to say that ... and how much he loved your hair."

Johnna was pensive. "That seems so long ago ...

another world. But now ... the memories are good, even comforting, not painful like they were." Turning to face her daughter, Johnna said, "Jess, I always will love your father, the life we had was precious, and all that is stored away for safe-keeping. But I'm feeling content in the here-and-now, knowing you are positive about your future and Charlie is just a happy little boy with his dog."

Jess hugged her mother and gave her a kiss on the cheek. "Well, Gorgeous, I think you are ready."

With Max close behind, Charlie entered the room and climbed into Johnna's lap. Patting her cheek, he said, "Mommy, you look pretty. Can I go too?"

"No, sweetie, you're going to stay here with Max and Grandma and Jess. This is just for grownups."

"Just you and Mr. Luke?" Charlie asked.

"Yes, just Mommy and Mr. Luke."

Charlie jumped from his mother's lap and ran into the kitchen, where they heard him say, "Grandma, Mommy and Mr. Luke are grownups. We can't go."

When Luke knocked on the front door, Johnna answered and said, "I guess a knock is somewhere between ringing the doorbell and sticking your head in to ask if we're all decent."

"Yeah, I didn't want to be formal, but it's not exactly a night at the bowling alley either." He whistled. "By the way, you look gorgeous."

For a moment, Johnna was speechless. "Well ... you clean up well yourself. I think my daughter would say that's a 'fire' outfit."

Jess came into the foyer and said, "Oh, yeah, no forest ranger drab," she agreed, admiring his neat jeans, crisp white shirt, and navy blazer. "And look, you've got sharp loafers, not boots."

"I have had a life outside of the trees, Jess," he declared. "Now, enough fashion show. We've got dinner reservations, and I'm starving."

From the kitchen, Lily called, "Oh, wait, wait." With Charlie and Max at her heels, she came rushing to the foyer with her phone, saying, "Let me take some pictures."

Johnna protested, "Oh, Mom, please, we're not teenagers on a first date."

"No, you're not spring chickens," she laughed, snapping several shots, "but this is a first date."

"Okay, we're out of here," Luke declared. "Johnna, are your shoes comfortable? I thought we'd park near the restaurant and then walk over the bridge to the concert, about half a mile there and back."

"Oh, sure. I'm good to go." Johnna gave Charlie a kiss and said, "Love you, sweetie." To Jess and her mother, Johnna said, "Love you guys. Don't wait up for us."

Lily winked at her granddaughter. "We won't … unless we just can't sleep."

Luke and Johnna left the restaurant and began the popular lighted walk to the concert. "That food was amazing, Luke—and all you can eat! I guess one difference between a first date at seventeen and a first date at thirty-seven is, at thirty-seven, you just feel free to eat and seriously enjoy the food, without reservation."

"We were well-mannered, though, don't you think?" he joked.

"Oh, yes, very decorous, to use one of Jess' big words—no slurping or burping, and nothing left hanging in our teeth, I trust," she said with a broad toothy smile.

"You're fine. How about me?" he asked, returning

the expression.

"A-okay," she stated.

"Let's go by the truck," Luke said. "I need to pick up a couple of things."

From the back seat, Luke took a tote bag and handed it to Johnna. "And this is?" she asked.

"That's dessert. I trust you like chocolate-covered strawberries."

"Whoa, 'How much?' is the question."

"A couple of bottles of water in there too," he added, retrieving a rolled quilt. "And this ... our reserved seating," he stated.

Johnna laughed, "Well, after all I've eaten, including dessert, my seating will be very comfortable."

It seemed natural for Luke to take her hand as they walked. "I'd forgotten how beautiful the promenade across the river is in the evening," she remarked.

"It's even more beautiful tonight with you here," he smiled.

"Why, Luke Ferguson, what a nice thing to say. I believe you have a romantic streak."

"I guess it's still there," he chuckled. "It hasn't surfaced in a long time."

"I don't want to be nosey," Johnna ventured, "but is there a 'Mrs. Ferguson' in your past?"

"There was almost one ... out West. I had invested money in a ring and hope in a future, but ... well, it just wasn't to be. Our visions for our life together were too different. It wouldn't have worked ... we both knew it."

"I'm sorry. It had to be hard ... for both of you."

"Yeah, for a while. But coming back home helped ... my work helped. And your mother ... well, she is the 'GOAT,'" he declared.

"My mother, a goat? You'll have to explain that one."

"Jess needs to bring you up to speed—'Greatest Of All Time.'"

As they sat on the knoll overlooking the concert stage, Johnna wondered how an evening could be any better than this. For the first time in so long, she was completely relaxed and warm in the curve of Luke's embrace. "Rhapsody in Blue" had just finished, when Luke asked, "Think we could do this again?"

"Only if you bring more strawberries," she teased.

"I might be able to manage that," he replied and gave her a kiss on the cheek.

When he laughed, Johnna asked, "What's so funny?"

"I just got chocolate on your face."

As she took a tissue from her bag, she noticed: "You do have a little blob right there" and dabbed his chin with her tissue.

Chapter 43

A little nervous and a lot excited, Jess pulled her hair back with the silver chain ponytail holder she had admired at the mall. She had dressed in dusty blue cargo pants and a tie-dyed elbow-sleeve tee with shades of blue and gray that accentuated her eyes. The cushy new espadrilles on her feet revealed pedicured toes matching manicured pink nails, on which her mother had insisted during their "girls' day out" shopping trip. The ID badge was clipped to her shirt, and her backpack was ready—Air Book, charging cable, water bottle, planner, notebook, pens, and pencils.

Entering the room, her mother asked, "Have you got everything? Calliope should be pulling up any minute now."

"I think so." Reviewing what she had packed, she concluded: "My phone wallet is in the outer pocket of the book bag. I've got the debit card, in case I need to buy textbooks at the campus store ... lunch money... and phone, of course. Anything else?"

"Sounds like you've got it together," Johnna replied. Opening her arms to her daughter, Johnna said, "Come ... give me a hug." As she embraced Jess, her mother said, "I pray this will be a wonderful day. I'm so proud of you. Just remember who you are—make us proud but be the person you are supposed to be—honest, caring, industrious ... always doing right, even if everyone else is doing wrong."

"Mom, I promise ... I've got all that." She chuckled, "Just say a prayer for our getting to school safely with Callie's driving."

Grandma and Charlie met Jess and Johnna at the front door. Handing her a bag of cookies, Lily said, "These are for you and Callie. Tell her she's invited to eat dinner with us this evening. Hope you have a good day, dear."

"Thanks, Grandma. We'll save these for an afterschool treat."

Charlie pulled on Jess' shirt. "Charlie give Sissy a kiss."

Jess stooped to allow him to buss her cheek, and he said, "I love you, Jess."

She noted he used her given name, and she struggled with emotion, as she replied, "Charlie, I love you, too, little brother."

They heard Calliope's car horn in the driveway, and Jess closed the door behind her with "I love you" ricocheting through the foyer.

"Good morning, Calliope," Jess greeted, as she set the backpack on the passenger side floorboard.

"'Departing summer hath assumed, An aspect tenderly illumed' ... Wordsworth."

"You always seem to pull the most fitting poem for any occasion from your cerebral collection," Jess observed, smiling at Calliope and receiving no response. "I appreciate the ride this morning. Mom said, if you finish before my last class, she can pick me up."

"That won't be necessary. I have work to do. Just come to my office in the Humanities building when you're ready to leave."

"Well, thanks again." As they passed over the Downtown Bridge, Jess observed along the river the wealth of construction projects in various stages of completion. The city was becoming more than a tourist-magnet, but a settlement of upscale homes for deep-pocketed homeowners, who could afford to live in the burgeoning social and cultural scene of the city.

"What classes do you have today?" Calliope ventured a question.

Raising her eyebrows at the unexpected opening of communication, Jess answered: "Well ... I tested out of seventh grade math and Language Arts, so ... Algebra 1, American Literature, General Science, and Social Studies. I have a Spanish lab session to see if I can pass First Year and go to Second. I've got Bible History and Geography as an elective, and a phys. ed. class that, today, is just going on a walking tour of the campus and the old city cemetery."

"You have a full schedule," she observed.

"Well, phys. ed. only meets three days a week, and I'll have a free period the other two days. I love school and learning. I just hope the classes are interesting."

"Teaching is the focus of the instructors in this program—not the stipend. They applied because of their desire to teach and were selected based on student reviews. You should be well-satisfied with the classes. You will be in my class next year—'British Literature and Poetry.'"

Jess replied, "I'll look forward to that," though she could not imagine Calliope's persona as a popular college professor.

As they parked in the faculty lot and Jess exited the vehicle, she noticed Calliope had settled "Old Blue" outside of her allotted boundary and wondered if the assignee of that next space would be able to adjust. "Have a good day, Calliope. I'll meet you in your office."

"Humanities, Room 324," Calliope responded, as she took a weathered leather shoulder satchel from behind the front seat. Jess noticed Calliope looked much like she did the first time Jess saw her, on the rock, only today a brown paisley maxi-skirt had replaced the jeans. The old safari hat topped the braiding of long dark hair, the denim jacket covered a brown tee shirt, and she was wearing the same old boots. Calliope, obviously, was indifferent to make-up, jewelry, or other embellishments—or summer clothes when the temperature still called for them. *She can't hide how naturally pretty she is,* Jess thought.

Thus far, the first full day of the TSP was everything Jess had hoped. The classes had been interesting, the teachers cordial, and the students polite, if a bit distant. Jess assumed her fellow classmates, like herself, were "getting the lay of the land," as Grandma sometimes said. Perhaps, they, also, were wondering if there would be time to spare for extended social interaction—their backpacks were heavy with texts and assignments for every course. Thankful for the assignment of lockers before phys. ed., they enjoyed the casual association of the walking tour, late in the afternoon before the last class—for Jess, her Bible History and Geography elective.

Jess entered a small, dimmed lecture hall, where classical music filtered around rows of tablet-armed chairs, cushioned for comfort. The soft melodies accompanied a slide show at the front of the hall, where appeared scenes of beautiful landscapes and places of geographical and historical interest. A note accompanied each slide to identify the location of the scene and the musical piece accompanying it—Pachelbel, Debussy, Chopin, etc. Jess thought, *I'm supposed to stay awake for this class?*

Jess surveyed the room, noting there were only six other students. She smiled to imagine all of them so completely relaxed, they passed out asprawl in their desks. When the teacher entered from the side door of the hall, she was surprised to recognize Steve Daniels, whose son was at Charlie's birthday party. "Good afternoon, class. I am Professor Daniels. I will be your instructor for Bible History and Geography. I am an adjunct professor here, teaching, as needed, in the areas of the Classics and Ancient History.

The slide show, the music, and Professor Daniels' soothing voice were hypnotic. But, rather than soporific, they invigorated her mind like a dry sponge thirsty for hydration. For Jess, the class was over far too soon, and she felt compelled to tell Mr. Daniels her eagerness for the next session. "Professor Daniels, you may not remember me …"

"Oh, yes, you're Charlie's sister and my co-sitter for a tangle of small children and a dog," he laughed.

"Yes, sir. I was surprised to see you're teaching this class, but I want to tell you how much I enjoyed it. It passed by far too quickly. Thank you. I look forward to tomorrow."

"Well, thank you for the positive feedback."

"Well, good afternoon, sir. I'll see you tomorrow."

Jess had turned to leave the hall, when Mr. Daniels asked, "Is your mother picking you up this afternoon?"

"Oh, no, sir. I'm meeting my friend, Professor Winchester, in the Humanities building and riding home with her."

"Would that be Calliope Winchester, the friend I met at the party?"

"Yes, sir. She teaches here."

"Hmm … I've never run into her … but then, I'm only an adjunct, not full-time."

"Well, see you tomorrow, sir," Jess called as she made her way up the ramp to the double doors.

"Jess!" Mr. Daniels stopped her. "Let me gather my things, and I'll join you. I'd like to see Miss Winchester. I may owe her an apology." Jess was puzzled but waited for Daniels to accompany her to Calliope's office. As they walked, he continued: "I must have said something to offend her at the party. We were talking on the porch, and she suddenly left and went over the hill … to her cabin, I assume."

Jess proceeded carefully: "Mr. Daniels, Calliope … Professor Winchester, is a little eccentric. She is uncomfortable around new people or in situations she finds confusing. She is so intelligent and knows so much about poetry, literature, and things in her field. But … she tends to be reclusive … at times, even naive."

"Hmm … you may be interested to know a college setting like this is a harbor for many such vessels."

Jess laughed, "You sound like Calliope. She has a poem or poetic expression for every situation".

They walked up to the third floor of the Humanities building and knocked on the door of Room 324. "Jess, if that's you, come in."

Opening the door, Jess announced, "It's me … and Professor Daniels."

Calliope looked puzzled.

Steve Daniels moved to shake Calliope's hand. "I met you at Charlie's birthday party. I sat with you on the porch."

Calliope said, "Sit down," and motioned to the chairs in front of her desk.

Daniels continued: "I want to apologize if I offended you that day … if I said something to upset you … you left suddenly … in a hurry, it seemed."

"I don't remember," Calliope responded. "If it makes you feel better, apology accepted."

Jess noticed the scarcity of books on the shelves and observed, "Calliope, this is nothing like your office at home." Turning to Steve Daniels, she added, "Her library at home is like a warm cocoon lined with hundreds of catalogued volumes of poetry and literature, much of which Calliope has committed to memory."

Calliope began, "'They stand together row by row, upon the low shelf or the high….'"

And Daniels completed the stanza: "But if you're lonesome this you know: You have a friend or two nearby.'…Guest." He continued: "'There is no frigate like a book to take us lands away, nor any coursers like a page of prancing poetry.'"

"Dickinson." Calliope's voice was soft in response.

"Yes … succinct and so true. Of course, my library includes history, geography—primarily Biblical, but also classic literature and poetry." He chuckled, remembering: "My late wife said she never had to fear my attraction to another woman, but there was always the threat of a rare book."

Calliope folded her laptop, collected her notes, and stuffed her belongings into the old brown satchel. "It's time to go, Jess."

Standing to leave, Daniels agreed, "Yes, I must pick up Alex at preschool." Before allowing the door to close behind him, he stated: "Miss Winchester, I would very much like to see your book collection when Alex has a play date with Charlie. Jess might accompany me, if agreeable to both of you."

"We'll see" was Calliope's terse response.

"Well ... then ... good afternoon," he said, nodding to Jess.

Chapter 44

The late Saturday afternoon in early fall was temperate, with a gentle breeze rustling the trees and stirring the lashes on Calliope's drowsy face, as she lounged in the porch rocker. The heavy tome of Shakespeare's Tragedies fell open on her lap, as she faded from thoughts of Gertrude's words to Hamlet, in Act 1, Scene 2: "Thou know'st 'tis common; all that lives must die, Passing through nature to eternity."

As usual, today's meditation had brought no new understanding of the cloak of mourning that had enveloped her inner being for years since Jeff's loss. Of course, she understood the normal aging and dying of every living thing—even when death, like Jeff's, had come as the result of a sudden tragic ending of physical processes. But she could not conquer her fear of leaving the world in which his death held her captive. He had made her secure, comfortable, surrounded by things she knew and understood ... that understood her—her books, his drawings, and the memories preserved in precious photos on a mantel Jeff had carved with his own hands. Outside this world, she was a foreigner in a land where she did not fully understand the customs, language, or expectations. She might function in its society, but they were unaware she was an alien, awaiting her own inevitable termination.

"Calliope!" Jess jarred Calliope from her slumber. Following the sound of her voice, she saw Jess and Steve Daniels exiting the trail to Lily's house. "I'm glad we're finding you at home."

Calliope thought, *Where else would you find me?*

Jess ascended the steps. "Grandma sent you some food. Alex came to play and eat supper with Charlie, so we grilled some hamburgers and hotdogs." Handing the plate to Calliope, she continued, "There's one of each, plus some baked beans and slaw. That's a brownie wrapped separately on top."

"Thank you ... neighborly of you" was Calliope's perfunctory remark.

"Calliope, would you mind showing Mr. Daniels your office? I have told him what a great place it is."

Rising from her station, Calliope said, "Come in."

Daniels scaled the steps, saying, "Thank you, Miss Winchester. I am very interested in seeing your collection."

"Let me put this food away first," she replied, heading toward the refrigerator.

Looking around the cabin, Daniels remarked, "This is a beautiful cabin."

Jess said, "My uncle Jeff designed it." Pointing to the drawings around the wall, she continued: "Uncle Jeff drew these."

"They are wonderful—very impressive," he observed.

Jess added, "I never really knew him, but I have heard he was a good man and a talented architect."

Calliope interrupted their conversation, walking between them to lead Jess and Daniels back to her office. Calliope stood at the door while Jess led Mr. Daniels into her inner sanctum.

"What a wonderful place!" he exclaimed. "I could live in here, wrapped in thousands of words and thoughts erupting from the minds of mortal men, made in the image of their Immortal Creator!" He pulled glasses from his shirt pocket and adjusted them to read the spine labels, moving his index finger from one book to the next. For minutes, he surveyed the shelves, absorbed with an interest that lost time and awareness of the presence of others. Finally speaking, he asked, "Miss Winchester, I wonder if you would share your catalog with me? And I would like for you to visit my own library sometime. I would be happy to share my catalog with you. Perhaps, we could have a friendly, informal … yet secure, sharing arrangement. You have some volumes I would very much like to access, and I think you would find some in my collection interesting, some even rare. You obviously care for your books like the good friends they are—I would trust you with my friends, also."

Jess was amazed by Calliope's tender expression, as she replied, "Good books are friendly things to own." Jess laughed when Calliope and Mr. Daniels said in unison, "Edgar A. Guest."

Calliope went to her desk and took a USB drive from the drawer. Handing it to Steve Daniels, she said, "Here, this is an extra copy. I haven't added anything new since I updated that."

"Thank you, Miss Winchester. This is much appreciated," he gestured with the drive before pocketing it. "Perhaps after school one day … soon, you and Jess can come by our house and peruse my collection."

"I would like to do that," she replied, adding: "You may call me Calliope."

Chapter 45

"Thou comest, Autumn, heralded by the rain ..."
Johnna was reminded of Calliope's words during the rains that fell ... so long ago now, it seemed. Thus far, October was dry, the leaves falling dead and lifeless without any colorful "last hurrah" before winter. Maybe next year, she thought. She remembered so many years in her childhood when the people of the valley anticipated rejoicing in the beauty of autumn colors and wishing for deep velvet blankets of winter snow—no ice, please, but thick white snow that promised sledding, snow cream, and cozy, hot cocoa-filled evenings gathered with family around the fireplace.

Johnna heard the door close and turned to see Lily coming to join her on the porch step, with mug in hand. "How about a decaf mocha cappuccino for dessert?" Lily asked, offering her the cup.

"Ooh, fancy! Sure," Johnna replied. "Thanks, but you shouldn't have gone to the trouble."

"No trouble," her mother laughed, "The little package said: 'Decaf Mocha Cappuccino—just add hot water and stir.'" Lily sat next to her daughter and observed, "Not a very cheery fall for you, is it?"

"Not as colorful as I had hoped."

"Luke said they've got extra crew not only manning the fire tower around the clock, but patrolling the preserve to enforce fire restrictions and monitor any suspicious activity. Sad to say, but California hasn't cornered the market on crazies," she teased.

Wistful, Johnna said, "Yes, he said he couldn't be around much until this Fire Danger Period is over," Johnna said.

"It's a 'Total Fire Ban' now," Lily replied. "I just heard it on the news. Tomorrow we'll make sure we have hoses on all the faucets in case we have to wet the roof. We've tried to keep a fire break cleared between us and the tree line, but if we have a burn like we did when you were young, those embers can travel and do serious damage."

"I remember being so scared ... seeing the flames so close behind us—and I was crying because I was afraid for all the animals in the woods."

"Yes, I know ... so was Jeff ... two inconsolable children, while your dad frantically tried to keep water on everything and I packed a 'go box,' just in case we had to evacuate. I remember working like an adrenaline-fueled machine to keep you children contented—and corralled, while I gathered documents, valuables, photo albums, medications ... and, of course," she smiled to remember, "my cosmetics bag."

Johnna sighed, "Mom, there are times I think about Luke's work ... the 'rangering,' if that's what you'd call it ..." She looked at Lily as if to admonish her: "... his little deputy sideline so he can chase bad guys. ... I don't know ... There's that risk of danger, and I've had more than I care to remember of waiting and praying my guy returns home at the end of the day. Luke is getting serious about this relationship, and I know how I feel about him. ... I just don't know if I can put myself or the children back in a situation where we might have to endure again that kind of loss ... the excruciating sadness, the grief."

They rocked in pensive silence for some moments,

then Lily asked: "Just assuming Luke might ask you to marry him at some point … and you turned him down out of fear of losing him … given his relationship to us—like one of the family, would you feel his loss any less if you were not married? You'd still love him. The children would still love him. Would it hurt any less if he were simply 'our close friend like a brother, Luke,' rather than 'husband and stepdad, Luke'?"

"Oh, mom … you make it all sound so simple."

"And, Johnna, dear, seems to me you're making it hard on yourself—trying to live in the past, present, and future all at the same time. You can't change the past, and the future is only our best efforts in the present, with the blessings and challenges only God knows we'll need. 'This is the day the Lord has made; We will rejoice and be glad in it.' It's simply not right to avoid the here and now, for fear it will be like yesterday or may result in an unpleasant tomorrow. 'Carpe Diem,' 'Tempus Fugit' … all that other stuff Callie might say."

Laughing, Johnna shook her head in resignation. "Then, there's Callie. I wonder how she might feel about, in a sense, losing Luke."

"She wouldn't be 'losing' Luke. He would be just as much a presence in her life as he is now—just not sleeping in her loft." Lily continued: "This is as good a time as any to tell you what I've been thinking. Of course, I'm assuming you and Luke move ahead in this relationship. You know this property is to be yours when I'm gone. Well, I would go ahead and deed it to you and Luke as my wedding gift, and I would move into the cabin with Callie. I'd take the monk's cell," she quipped, "as my bedroom, and she'd have the loft. The office is all that's precious to her. This house would be ideal for you and Luke; the children would each have a bedroom, and you and Luke, your own private annex."

"Well, you've been doing a lot of thinking," Johnna declared. "Is this all just some scenario you've had playing in your head while you've been standing over a hot stove—or do you have inside information I don't know about?"

Lily grinned. "I am just a perceptive mother, who, at times, knows her children better than they know themselves." Lily took Johnna's hand: "And I pray your life will be happy and good and … beautiful."

Chapter 46

"Good afternoon, Jess, and Calliope … I'm so pleased you accepted my invitation to come by."

Alex joined his father at the door, and Jess said, "Hi, Alex. Charlie said to tell you he wants you to come again soon to our house to play with him. He had lots of fun."

"I want to see Max and Fritz, too," he responded.

Steve Daniels asked, "Alex, do you remember Miss Winchester? She was at Charlie's birthday party."

Jess was amused at Calliope's befuddled expression, when Alex shook her hand and said, "You're the pretty lady who gave Charlie the puppy."

"Please, come in, come in," Mr. Daniels encouraged them, as he directed them into the living room. "Would you like something to drink?"

"None for me," answered Callie.

"No, thanks. I'm fine, too," Jess agreed.

"Alex, why don't you go play in your room while I show Jess and Miss Winchester my office?"

Alex started toward his bedroom, then turned to say, "Jess, come see my room. I have an orrery."

Mr. Daniels clarified the term for Jess: "That's a new word he's learned. It's a model of the solar system."

"I'll be there in just a few minutes," she replied, smiling at the precocious four-year-old.

They passed through the living and dining rooms, a neat white kitchen, and a plant-filled sunroom, that connected the main house to a double garage. Carpeted stairs just inside the garage door rose to a second-floor apartment, entirely given to Daniels' office and library—an impressive space, designed for functionality, comfort, and aesthetic appeal. Custom-made, ceiling height white bookshelves, filled with volumes—some accessed by a rolling library ladder, surrounded a conversational grouping in proximity to a fireplace with white surround and mantel graced by a framed map of the ancient world. A spacious cherry desk and brown leather executive chair faced two matching leather armchairs flanking a vintage drum table. A Turkish rug in a pattern of red, sage green, and beige grounded the pieces of furniture and complemented the sage green ceiling and random strips of sage green wall appearing between bookcases and around windows.

"What a beautiful place!" Jess exclaimed, as Calliope circled the room, gently grazing books and furniture, as if laying a blessing on each item.

"Why, thank you, Jess. I am rather proud of my little world. I did most of the work myself. I have a small woodworking shop downstairs, so I saved a great deal of money on the shelves … on that ceiling height storage cabinet," he said, pointing to its position in the corner of the room, "… and on the faux fireplace surround. It's electric, you see."

In front of a glass doored offset section of cases, shielded from windows and direct sunlight, Calliope stood frozen, except for the flutter of her hands at her side. "You have a first edition of Longfellow's Poems," she stated.

"Yes, the signature is tipped in, but it's Longfellow's, nonetheless. I have several other first editions there and a handful of rare books you'll find interesting."

Jess commented, "Mr. Daniels, I think you have set Calliope free in a candy store."

"I must admit, I share the sentiment. I am forever amazed at the momentous wealth of creativity with which God has gifted men down through the ages. Of course, sometimes I think entropy pertains even to humanity's moral and ethical standards and is inhibiting the production of new great literary works. Those which have passed the test of time, in my opinion, spring from man's innate spiritual nature, not from his baser proclivities."

Jess laughed and said, "Mr. Daniels, you have given me quite a few new vocabulary words to add to my list."

"Ha, Jess! I guess I have," he chuckled.

"Mr. Daniels, if you don't mind, I'll leave you and Calliope to talk, and I'll go see Alex. He's expecting me."

"Sure, Jess. You can find your way?"

"Oh, yes. I'll be there when Calliope is ready to leave."

"Do you have a certain time you must be home?" Daniels asked.

"Oh, no, just in time for dinner about six o'clock or so," she replied, as she crossed to the staircase. You guys take your time."

Chapter 47

Taking a USB drive from a leaf-shaped tray on his desk, Daniels approached Calliope and said, "This is a copy of my catalogue for you. Any time you'd like to borrow a book—or if you would like to come here and make use of the library, just give me a call ... or catch me before or after my TSP class. I'd be happy to make the arrangement with you."

Returning her gaze to the shelves, Calliope stated: "My collection is not as extensive as yours. I have more poetry and literature, and you have more history and geography."

"They are closely interconnected disciplines. Man's desire to express himself through poetry and prose springs from his soul, in reaction to his environs and his experiences within it. Have you ever tried your hand at writing your own poetry, Miss Winchester ... Calliope?"

She responded: "My soul does not sing, but hums, With measured notes, discordant."

"I assume that's your verse?"

"My poetry is self-centered, self-analytical, for want of understanding myself. It has no literary or amusement value."

"Calliope, that may be ascertained only by one's reader. You are a unique person, very interesting and engaging in a way that sets you apart from the mass of ordinary people, who hear only with their ears and not their hearts."

"Professor Daniels, may I consider you my friend?" Calliope was earnest, childlike in her request.

"Most assuredly, Calliope, and, please, call me Steve. I am in the business of caring for souls and helping them to understand and care for themselves. Maybe our friendship can be encouraging and enlightening for both of us. Remember Longfellow's words: 'And the song, from beginning to end, I found again in the heart of a friend.'"

As usual on the way home, Calliope was in quiet communion with her own thoughts, when Jess asked, "What did you think of Professor Daniels' office?"

"It is a fitting place for such a man as Steve Daniels. Wordsworth said, 'Great men have been among us; hands that penned and tongues that uttered wisdom ...' He is a wise man and a good friend."

"He preaches and teaches where we worship. His lessons have helped me a lot. I was so angry when Dad died—angry at Mother, mainly ... but it wasn't her fault. It was nobody's fault. Maybe I really was angry at God for letting it happen, but even God would not keep Dad from doing what he wanted to do ... what his work required him to do."

"Every choice has an outcome," Calliope stated. "Your Dad made the choice to go to work that day. His work had two potential outcomes—life or death. That day, the outcome was death."

Jess sighed and said, "That's about the short of it, Calliope." Jess considered her words carefully before proceeding, "Calliope, what happened to you the day Uncle Jeff died?"

Calliope sorted through the files of her memory until she returned to the day of the accident. "I was teaching when Luke came into my classroom and told my students they were excused for the rest of the period. He said there would be a posting on the door about the next meeting. I didn't understand how he could do that—just tell my class to leave. He told me to sit down, so I sat down in my desk chair. I knew he and Jeff were hunting that morning. They were in the woods when Jeff accidentally shot himself in the femoral artery. Luke used his belt for a tourniquet and carried him back to the truck and then to the hospital. But Jeff lost too much blood, and he died."

"What did you do, then?" Jess asked.

"Luke took me back to the cabin. I waited for Jeff, but he didn't come." Calliope's voice faded as she said, "He never has come."

"Calliope, he won't come back, and my dad won't either. Like Mr. Daniels said in one of his lessons, 'Now he is dead ... Can I bring him back again? I shall go to him, but he shall not return to me.' I know now I must make the most of my life and stop thinking I can bring back the old one when Dad was alive."

Calliope said, "I know. No one had to post a note. I taught my class the next day—we discussed the foreshadowing in Romeo and Juliet."

Chapter 48

Johnna was deep in early morning sleep when Max's whimpering and Charlie's voice began chipping through the barrier of her unconsciousness. "Mommy, mommy, Max won't be quiet." She sat up and could sense the faintest smell of smoke. Opening the door to their bedroom, Max rushed out the door to the annex, where he scratched at Lily's door and whined at the sound of Fritz's barking. Soon Lily was throwing on her housecoat and rushing down the hallway to meet Johnna. "We've got smoke coming from somewhere. Get the children out on the porch until we see what's going on."

Johnna hurried to wake Jess. "Jess … Jess! Get up! Get Charlie and come outside on the porch. There's smoke coming from somewhere."

Jess slipped her feet into her house shoes and ran to pick up Charlie from his bed.

As Lily opened the front door, Fritz and Max raced out, nearly knocking her from her feet. "Let me get my boots," Lily shouted, "and I'll go around and check the roof."

"Mom, look!" Johnna cried. "Up there!" There was fire at the tree line, up the rise behind the mini barn.

As the dogs barked and whirled in agitation, Lily ordered: "Jess, stay out here with Charlie and Max. Johnna, go around the house and make sure you soak everything with the hoses. I'm going down the road to get Calliope. Luke's prepared her, but she's closer to the flames than we are." Heading back to the house to get her keys to the Jeep, she signaled to Max to "Stay!" and ordered, "Fritz, come!"

Lily gunned the Jeep as she maneuvered the curves to the cabin and prayed all would be well with Callie and Luke. She knew Johnna and the children were secure at the house, but she would not rest until she knew everyone in her family was safe and out of the reach of the greedy, licking tongues of flame.

Lily pulled off the road at the foot of the lane. Running up the porch steps and pounding on the door of the cabin, Lily received no response. Then, she heard Fritz's frantic barking and followed the sound to the rear of the cabin, where Callie, standing in a mire of mud and hissing steam, was dousing a hollowed corner of the structure and fighting a hungry enemy that refused to cease its attempts to feast on her precious books.

Seizing the hose from Callie, Lily ordered, "Go save what you can inside. ... Fritz, go with Callie!" Lily struggled to defeat the last spark, until nothing was left but the blackness of soot and ruin. Weary, she staggered back, nearly losing her footing and falling in the muck. "Callie!" she called. "It's out ... it's ..." Then, the section of roof collapsed into the cabin.

With a renewed surge of energy, Lily raced around the cabin and bounded up the porch. She found Fritz, jaws clenched on the denim jacket Callie had thrown over her nightdress—he was pulling her, apparently unconscious, from the smoldering heat of the wreckage that had been her office. Lily added her remaining strength to Fritz's effort, thankful that Callie was small and Fritz was still powerful and resolute.

They had managed to get Callie securely outside

the office and Lily was checking her breathing, when Luke bounded into the cabin, "Is she ...? He began.

"She's alive but unconscious. I think a beam must have hit her when the back part of the roof caved in." As Luke checked her pulse and reflexes, Lily asked, "What are you doing here?"

"We spotted the outbreak. There are crews working on it now." Luke called for medical assistance on his two-way, then stabilized Callie's head and neck with rolled towels from the bathroom. "Just a precaution," he said. "Her reflexes seem to be okay, but we can't move her till the techs arrive. She has some burns, but I think nothing serious."

With her hand on the head of the loyal companion next to her, Lily watched as the EMTs loaded Callie into the ambulance and the siren began to wail. Luke had said, "Go ... take care of Johnna and the kids," before proceeding in his truck behind the emergency vehicle. The nearest ER was only nine miles away—from there, if necessary, the helicopter could take Callie to the medical center downtown.

Lily said, "Fritz, let's see if we can salvage anything before we close up." The office appeared a total loss, but only smoke affected the remainder of the cabin, now open and vulnerable to mischief. Lily found Callie's purse on the chair in her bedroom, along with her key ring. Next to the bed was Callie's satchel, from which she apparently had taken a book, now on the nightstand. Gathering books and clothes to wash for Callie's wearing in the days ahead, Lily headed toward the door. "Oh, Fritz, I've got to get some things for Luke, too." Dropping what she had collected on the couch, she went upstairs and scoured the space for anything Luke might want held in her safekeeping. She took familiar clothes from his closet and underclothes from his dresser drawers—she'd make sure they were clean and ready for his wearing. Opening a valet box on the top of the dresser, she saw it contained what appeared to be official documents, some cash, extra keys ... and ... a ring box. She took the small velvet container from its place and opened it to reveal an emerald-cut diamond, flanked on one side by a blue sapphire, and on the other, by a pink sapphire. She thought, I know what that's about and returned it to its location.

Lily brought the box and clothes downstairs and added them to the collection on the couch. Looking around the cabin, she declared: "Fritz, I'm not going to allow Callie to lose her whole world"—she removed Jeff's drawings from the walls and loaded them in the back of the Jeep with the other things she had retrieved. She motioned for Fritz to get in the passenger's seat, telling him to "Stay." She went back to the cabin, partially opened the windows, and scanned the area once more. Oh, me, she thought as she looked toward the mantel, Callie's photographs!

Lily knew Johnna and the children, having witnessed the arrival and departure of the ambulance, would be waiting—awake, alert, and eager to know what had transpired.

Chapter 49

Johnna and Jess were waiting on the steps when Lily returned. Charlie and Max, now oblivious to their extraordinary predawn Friday, were playing in the yard in front of the porch. Lily pulled into the drive beside Johnna's vehicle. Jess watched as Fritz lowered himself to the ground, and her grandmother trudged up the walk with heavy, weary steps. Johnna went to her mother's side, taking her arm to support her. "Oh, Johnna, dear, I can make it. I'm just tired." Lily sat in a rocker, Fritz lay at her feet, she held her head in her hands, and tears began making spots on her blue pajama top.

"Mom, what's happened? We saw the ambulance." Lily recounted the events at the cabin, leading up to Callie's being whisked away to the hospital.

"Are you alright, Mom?"

"Oh, yes, I'm fine. You know how I am—I can hang together during the crisis, then after, I fall apart. I'm just so concerned about Calliope—her library is pretty much destroyed. I brought Jeff's drawings and her photographs for safe-keeping, but her life, her 'here and now,' was those books. I can't imagine the lasting impact this may have on her. She already was so … fragile."

"What can I do, Mom? Is there any way I can help?"

"We can all pray and wait, I guess, for Luke to get back to us with a report."

Jess said, "I can call Professor Daniels to let him know Calliope won't be able to teach today. He might be able to cover her class for her."

"I'm glad you thought of that, Jess," Johnna said. Looking at her watch, she added, "With the time difference, I'm sure he's up by now. Do you have his number?"

"Yes, he gave it to us the other day when we were at his house. He wanted Calliope to be able to get in touch with him to make appointments to use his library."

Johnna directed: "Go call him, and then get ready for school. You may be tired later, but you don't need to miss a day when all we can do is wait. Charlie and I will get ready, and we'll pick up some breakfast on the way. I'll take him to play group, so Grandma and I will be free if Luke needs us."

Jess was ready to end the call when she heard Mr. Daniels' voice: "Hello."

"Mr. Daniels, this is Jess McGregor. I apologize for calling so early."

"Good morning, Jess. No problem. I was just out of the shower and didn't hear the phone for a bit."

"Mr. Daniels, I will be at school later, but I wanted you to know Calliope has had an accident and won't be able to teach today. She will need someone to cover her class."

"Oh, no, Jess, what's happened?"

Jess recounted the early morning's events and waited for Mr. Daniels to respond.

"You say … she was unconscious? Do you know where she is—which hospital?" he asked.

"The last my grandmother knew, she was unconscious. She's probably at the ER in Mountain

Shadow. We haven't heard from her brother, Luke, so we don't know if she'll stay there or they'll take her to the Med Center."

"You say her library was a complete loss?"

"Grandma said it seemed so to her."

"Jess, this grieves me terribly. Please, feel free to call me whenever you have any news. Perhaps you will have an update when I see you at school this afternoon."

"Yes, sir. Thank you, sir. I'll see you later."

Jess ended the call and set about the laborious task of getting ready for school. She was up before four and would not return home until after five, and she knew much of that time would be occupied by thoughts of Calliope and her condition.

She had packed her backpack and was setting it by the front door, when she heard Lily answering her phone. "Hello ... Luke," she heard her grandmother say. "Any word yet?" Jess walked into the kitchen where her grandmother sat at the table with her coffee. Lily motioned Jess to join her to overhear the conversation. "Just a second, Luke. Jess just came in. Do you mind if I put us on speakerphone? ... Okay, now ... how is she?"

Jess thought Luke sounded drained of energy—he had been up all night on duty and now ... with Calliope's injury. "The doctors have taken x-rays and done scans. They have determined her head trauma is not life-threatening—no brain bleed, but they are puzzled that she has not regained consciousness. They will keep her here for a couple of days until she wakes up—if she doesn't, they'll run another battery of tests. Then, they may send her to the rehab unit of the nursing home."

"Oh, Luke, what can we do?"

"Just pray. That's all any of us can do right now."

"Luke, just a minute. ... Jess, go see if your mother

and Charlie are ready, and tell your mom what Luke has said."

Taking the phone off speaker, Lily lowered her voice. "Luke, do you think you ought to ask the doctors to call in a specialist? We both know Callie had issues before all this. I wonder if, after the trauma, part of her is choosing to stay unconscious?"

"Ms. Lily, you know, I wondered that myself when the doctors told me they were puzzled. Callie's world, literally and figuratively, has crashed down on her. ... Hey, Ms. Lily, I've got to run ... the doctor's here to speak to me. If there's any change, anything new, I'll call you."

"Thanks, Luke, please do. And, by the way, Luke, I brought what I could out of the cabin for safekeeping. You'll have clean clothes here."

"Oh ... Ms. Lily ... thank you ... for everything. You know I love you."

"No need to thank me, Luke—and I love you, too, dear."

Johnna entered the kitchen and said, "Mom, I'll take Jess to school and Charlie to play day. Then, I may go by the hospital and check on Luke, maybe take him something to eat."

"That's a good idea—seeing you is just what he needs right now."

Charlie ran to Lily and wrapped his arms around her legs. "Bye, Grandma. Love you."

"Have a good day, little man," she responded, hugging him to her.

Jess added, "Grandma, I'll see you after school. You need to try to get some rest today."

"I will, dear. I'm just going to do some laundry for Luke and Callie—get the smoke out if I can. Oh, and Luke, likely, will be sleeping on our couch this evening, so you girls keep your modesty in mind. We're not used to having a man in the house over the age of three."

"Love you, Grandma. See you later," Jess called as she went out the door.

"Mom, we'll keep in touch through the day. I won't plan to come home until after I pick Jess up."

Chapter 50

Thankful that Charlie had a safe and secure day ahead of him, Johnna gave her son a hug and kiss, left his snack and change of clothes in his cubby, and determined, rather than take Luke food, she would try to get him away from the hospital long enough to eat breakfast at the nearby diner. She might even persuade him to go to Lily's to rest and get cleaned up—he had to be exhausted.

"I'm Johnna McGregor," she told the hospital's receptionist. "My friend, Calliope Winchester, was admitted early this morning ..."

"Johnna." She hadn't noticed Steve Daniels, logging his name in the register nearby. He extended his hand and sandwiched hers in a warm gesture of care and compassion. "I'm so sorry about Calliope. I thought I might be able to help in some way."

"Good morning, Steve. Thank you. I'm hoping to get Luke away for a while. He's been up more than twenty-four hours and needs some food and rest."

"They only allow one person back there at a time. But, since they consider me 'CLERGY,'" he explained, tapping his I. D., "I can visit whenever. Apparently, I don't count as flesh, only spirit." She welcomed his effort to make her smile. "I'll see if Luke will let me relieve him. I'm free until later this afternoon and can sit with Calliope until one of you returns."

"Thanks—that would be very kind of you," she agreed. Johnna watched as Steve pushed the button to ask access of the nurses' station, and the double doors to the ward opened. Johnna sat, picked up a magazine, and thumbed through it, trying to still her racing thoughts. Again, she was amazed at how an ordinary day could become, almost instantly, a life-changing, mind-altering, history-changing point in one's life, with every detail etched in one's memory.

Though she didn't realize her function was set on "Record" the day J. B. was killed, she, even now, could remember the insignificant details of the day: She had thrown on her old gray sweats and pulled her hair back in a scrunchie. She fastened Charlie into his infant car seat, thankful for his contentment, and popped the baby's pacifier in his mouth. Jess held her brother's hand—so sweet, and he fell asleep while they drove to meet the carpool going into Bakersfield. *She's growing into a young lady—and so pretty.* Johnna had pulled Jess' hair up in a pearlized blue clip, as she had requested, to keep her thick brunette hair off her neck on what was already a sweltering morning. Johnna had been home only a few minutes, had put Charlie back in his baby bed, and was loading the breakfast plates into the dishwasher, when the doorbell rang. She opened the door to confront a notification officer in service uniform, behind whom stood their congregation's minister. "Mrs. J. B. McGregor?" the officer asked.

"Johnna, come sit down," the preacher directed, stepping into the living room and guiding her to the couch. "J. B. had put in his file a request for the base to contact me in case of emergency."

No, she thought, you have the wrong house. No, look at me. I'm a mess. I'm Jess and Charlie's mom. The officer continued: "Mrs. McGregor, the commander of Edwards Air Force Base has entrusted me to express his deep regret that your husband, Lieutenant Jonathan Burgess McGregor, was killed while on duty during flight testing yesterday ..." *No, you're mistaken. He's coming home this evening. We have a sitter. We have a date night—tickets to ...* "The commandant extends his deepest sympathy to you and your family in your time ..."

"Johnna." Luke tapped her on the shoulder, and she stood to wrap her arms around him. Johnna again felt secure in a present, which didn't guarantee there would be no storms, but that there would be shelter from them—and companionship when meeting their threats.

"Luke, is there any change?" she asked.

"No," he sighed. "She's still unconscious. Steve's with her now."

"Come, let's get you something to eat," she persuaded. "Maybe you can go to mother's and sleep for a while. I'll come back here and stay with Calliope until time to pick up Charlie."

"I guess I ought to," he replied, rubbing his head. "I won't be any good for anything if I don't get some rest. And," he laughed, "I know I smell something awful of smoke and sweat and scummy teeth."

She took his hand and pulled him toward the exit, "Well, that sounds a lot worse than the actual situation."

After their brunch, Johnna returned to the hospital and checked in at the reception desk. I'm a friend here to sit with Miss Winchester. May I go back?"

The nurse checked the chart on her desk and replied, "Yes, Mr. Ferguson said to consider you family. The minister is still in there, but he can be present at the same time you are—Room 187, through the doors, turn right, on the left at the end of the hall."

Johnna hadn't had much experience with hospitals,

but they all seemed to be the same—bustling activity in an antiseptic environment, where human voices were quiet, save for calls and codes on the speaker system. Signals beeped and pinged from machines that monitored the functions and rhythms of life, and the elevator announced its periodic landing with a chime and sliding of its doors.

Arriving at the room, Johnna peeked around the partially open door and saw Steve at Calliope's bedside. She hesitated when she heard his words: "Do you remember what Dickinson wrote about fire? 'Ashes denote that fire was; Respect the grayest pile, For the departed creature's sake That hovered there awhile.'" He was gripping Calliope's hand, as if to press life back into the stillness of her mind and body. "With sadness for its loss," he said, "we respect the memory of your beautiful space. But we can rebuild and replace it. I will help you. We have your catalog, and we will search and collect and make it even better than it was. We can find joy in the process. Remember, I am your friend." Picking up a book from his side, he said, "I brought this to read to you— Thoreau is one of my favorites." Johnna listened as Steve read a poem on friendship. She wondered, *How can he be so direct with his words, yet they're so kind and gentle?* He held Calliope's hand while reading. " ... For if the truth were known, Love cannot speak, But only thinks and does ..." *How touching, how perfectly fitting.* " ... When under kindred shape, like loves and hates And a kindred nature, Proclaim us to be mates, Exposed to equal fates Eternally; And each may other help, and service do ..."

Steve's words clarified Johnna's own feelings, when he read: " ... Two sturdy oaks I mean, which side by side, Withstand the winter's storm, And spite of wind and tide ... Their roots are intertwined Inseparably." She paused to consider her words, then knocked on the door.

"Good afternoon, Johnna," he said, standing. "Your timing is perfect. I must leave for the college. I'm going to cover Calliope's class before my own."

"Thank you, Steve, for sitting with her. Has there been any change?"

"None to see, but I know … I must believe … she hears me, and that she's just trying to decide if she wants to stay where she is, in her world as it was, or if there is enough love in this one to draw her back."

"Do you think I should talk to her … would that possibly help?"

"I don't know, but I have been told the unconscious can hear." Handing Johnna the book, he said, "You might read to her from this book of poetry. Words sometimes confuse her, I understand, unless they are organized in poetic style, rhythmic, aesthetic." He moved toward the door. "She is truly a beautiful, unique soul …" He left Johnna with an endearing smile and the words, "But then, each of us is."

Chapter 51

Lily was reading in front of the fireplace with Fritz by her side when Luke knocked on the door. Johnna and Jess had gone to bed early, thankful for the weekend ahead of them when they could recuperate from lack of sleep and the stress of the long day's events. A few catnaps during the day had allowed Lily to stay up to wait for the latest report from Luke.

"Come in, Luke," Lily said quietly. "Johnna and the children have called it a night."

"They've got to be tired," he responded. "I don't know if I could have survived without that shower and nap earlier."

"Any change in Callie's status?" Lily asked, returning to the armchair. Luke sat across from her on the couch, now made into a bed Lily knew he would find comfortable, even if he had to fold his lengthy frame to fit it."

"They'll keep her through Tuesday. Then, if she's not back among the living, they'll move her to the nursing home. Apparently, they feel there is no medical indication for her condition——they've confirmed the concussion was moderate, no bleeding, nothing that would cause physical unconsciousness this long. I told him our thoughts about a specialist, and they had the neurologist on call come by. He said he only knew what test results showed, but if there is an ASD—autistic spectrum disorder, associated with her injury, the trauma may cause some regression for a time, even depression, increased sensory sensitivity—noise, light ... He really couldn't help much right now."

"Luke, I've been thinking. Don't let them send her to the nursing home. If they want to discharge her Tuesday, bring her here. I can care for her—even help with therapy if they tell me what to do. She needs to be with family and in a place that's more familiar to her. I don't think rehab at some nursing home would be optimum for a person like Callie."

"I think you're right, Ms. Lily. Thank you. I would be forever grateful for your help."

"Well, you know, she should have been my daughter-in-law, but since that time, she's been my daughter-in-heart."

"You've been a mother to both of us for a long time now," he said, his eyes misting.

He rubbed them and continued: "Ms. Lily, I'm taking a leave of absence for a while, until I can get the cabin restored and Calliope is resettled, assuming she comes out of this state. I want to put her world back together."

"I pray the time comes soon," Lily told him.

Luke began to empty his pants pockets and lay items on the coffee table, when he remembered: "Oh, Ms. Lily, would you and Johnna be around for Charlie to play with Alex Daniels tomorrow? Steve's coming out later in the morning for us to assess what needs to be done at the cabin."

"That would be just fine. Charlie will be one happy little boy. ... But, Luke, I've been so concerned about Calliope I hadn't told you: Jeff had homeowner's insurance on that cabin ... on my policy, as another structure on our land. Of course, I've kept the coverage up-to-date. There'll be an adjustor out here Monday. I told him we must have the cabin restored as soon as humanly possible."

For the first time since Jeff's accident, Lily saw Luke in tears. She moved to sit next to him on the couch and put her arm around his broad back. Fritz came to sit in front of him and placed his paw on Luke's knee.

"Ms. Lily, I'm sorry," he apologized, taking his handkerchief from the coffee table to wipe his nose and face.

"Son, don't you ever apologize for tears—they are God's gift to cleanse a hurting heart. Emotions can overwhelm even big, strong guys like you—and God knows you've been storing up more than even you can handle. Remember: 'Those who sow in tears shall reap in joy.'" Lily stood and said, "Now, you get some rest. Sleep as long as you can in the morning. We'll keep Charlie at bay."

Luke smiled, "He's a special little guy. I look forward to spending more time with him. … Oh, Ms. Lily … did Johnna tell you Steve Daniels was with Calliope several hours today? From what I understand, they've become good friends—kind of kindred spirits. He wants to help rebuild her office and restore her library."

"He's such a good man. Jess was telling me about their visit to his house and library. She was 'super impressed'—her words," Lily smiled, "and Callie was 'virtually awe-struck'—again, her words. … Changing the subject, Luke, I put your clean clothes in the laundry closet, and your valet box is on the shelf inside the door. I must confess, when I was gathering stuff at the cabin, I looked in it to see if I should take it for safekeeping—of course, I saw that I should," she grinned.

"You know all my secrets now, don't you, Ms. Lily? … I've had plans working in my head ever since my

192

first date with Johnna. That was my first concrete step toward making them reality."

"Do you have any timeline in mind, if I'm not too bold to ask?"

"If you had asked me a couple of days ago, I would have laid it all out for you, but now … with the fire and Callie's injury … I don't know … things are up in the air. … Ms. Lily, just so you know—I don't want to worry Johnna and the children—I believe the fire at the cabin likely was arson. Considering the fire break between the cabin and the forest line and the speed with which the crew got the tree blaze under control, chances of it being a loose ember are slight. I'm thinking we may have one of Emory's gang giving a little payback on his behalf. Jack Collins had an arson investigator down at the cabin today. He'll be able to confirm my suspicions. With Emory and the two picked up at the restaurant, we feel sure one of them will snitch on the one we've missed. We may get him for arson and be able to increase the charges on Emory, if he masterminded it, and lock him away even longer."

"Do you think this place will be safe, Luke?"

"Well, like I said, Ms. Lily, I'm taking a leave of absence. I'll be around, and I think Emory's made his point, done his damage. Besides, you've got Fritz and now, Max. It's amazing how much respect some of these low-lifes have for dogs." He hesitated before continuing: "Johnna and Jess need to consider what a life with me would be … if they would want to be bound to someone who spends half his waking hours in Forest Law Enforcement—dealing with rattlesnakes, both human and reptilian." He shook his head and attempted a grin.

She observed, "Old 'Leonard What's-his-name?' did look like a slithery old snake." She confessed: "You know, Luke, that was fun—made me feel young and alive again. How about you, Fritz, my handsome boy?" she asked, petting the dog and feeling him lean against her. Lily said, "Well, again, good night. Come, Fritz, let's go to bed. Luke, sleep well. In the morning, I'll fix us a big 'Ranger breakfast'—or brunch. There are fresh towels in the bathroom. Anything you need you don't find in there may be in the pantry. Oh ... your robe and sleep pants are in the bathroom." Lily left with the parting words, "Rest well, Luke. It'll be nice to have you around for a while—I mean, really, around-around," she laughed.

Chapter 52

Johnna took the bag from the back seat of the SUV and accompanied Luke through the automatic doors to the reception desk. "We're here to see Calliope Winchester," he informed the receptionist. "I'm her brother, Luke Ferguson. She'll be checking out today. May we get permission for Mrs. McGregor to go back with me to help get her ready to go home?"

"The minister is with her now. I'll check. Just wait over there," the nurse said, directing them to nearby seats in the lobby.

Under her voice, Johnna said, "Last night at worship, Steve told me he was here for a couple of hours yesterday afternoon."

"And he left Charlie with us for a while Saturday so he could be here. He's really taken an interest in my little sister. I wonder if it's entirely spiritual?" he commented, leaning close to Johnna and raising his eyebrows.

Johnna giggled and replied, "It likely means nothing to her, but Calliope can't hide how pretty she is, even under that old hat and bohemian clothes."

"Mr. Ferguson," the nurse called, "you both may go on back."

Taking the bag, Johnna followed Luke down the long hallway to Calliope's room. Stopping at the door, Luke put his forefinger to his lips, then to his ear. Johnna heard Steve Daniel's resonant voice reading words to

Calliope: "My soul does not sing, but hums, with measured notes, discordant." Then, he said, "And this one I made with Longfellow's words: 'And the song, from beginning to end, I found again in the heart of a friend.' I apologize—I only had room for his initials, 'H. W. L.'"

"I like them very much" was Calliope's soft response.

Steve Daniels continued: "I thought, when we finish your office, you might find a space to hang them—your poetry right above Longfellow's," he announced.

Luke knocked on the door. "Good morning, Callie … Steve." Calliope was sitting upright in the hospital bed, and Luke took the opportunity to give his weakened sister a kiss on the cheek. "Did you decide to come back to us, Callie? We have waited and prayed for days for you to make up your mind. We've missed you."

"Steve made these for my new office," she said, indicating on her lap the polished wood plaques etched with fine script. "He is a good friend. He said I may use his library until mine is restored."

Johnna said, "That's wonderful. Steve, you have been a godsend, but," she laughed, "that's just your job description, isn't it?"

"God is the first and greatest poet, is He not, Calliope—from Whom spring all thoughts and beauty." To Luke, Steve said, "Your sister and I share a common love and appreciation of words." Laying his hand on Calliope's, he continued, "Though I know sometimes words fly around in your brain like leaves in a whirlwind, don't they, Calliope—especially now, since the sky fell on your head."

"Callie," Luke informed his sister, "we have brought clothes for you. Johnna will help you change, so we can take you to Lily's house. We'll stay there until the cabin is repaired."

"That's a good plan" was Calliope's simple reply.

Johnna placed the bag on Calliope's bedside table, directing the men to give them some time alone. ... "And, Luke, how about giving mother a call to tell her we're coming home? She and Jess and I have made plans for this day—she'll be happy it's come sooner rather than later. I'll text Jess to let her know, 'Operation Calliope' is underway."

Steve Daniels grasped Calliope's hand between his and said, "I'll check on you tomorrow. You get settled in at Lily's. Do you want me to take these to hold until your office is ready?"

"No, I'll keep them with me. Thank you for making them."

"You are very welcome." Daniels moved toward the door, saying, "I'll go on to the college. I'll see Jess later. I know she will be one happy girl."

Luke said, "I'll walk out with Steve, Johnna. Let me know when the nurse is here with the discharge papers."

"Will do," she replied. "Now, Calliope, let's see if what I brought is agreeable to you."

"Did you bring my hat ... and my jacket?" she asked.

Chapter 53

Lily had navigated between Charlie, his little people, his 'wild things people,'and Max, to put things in best order for Callie. She appreciated Jess' willingness to give up her personal space, and she hoped the whole process would be the beginning of several alterations over the coming months—not just residential, but relationship changes. She planned to stay on top of things at the cabin—getting the construction people in there for speedy, yet sound repairs and taking advantage of the situation to renovate the kitchen to accommodate more extensive meal preparation for six people … and changing bathroom fixtures to suit the needs of a woman approaching "threescore and ten." Also, she would venture to make the loft area more than the monk's cell that had been Calliope's recent downstairs bedroom … keeping it simple, but functional, peaceful, and attractive. *Why am I so excited?* she wondered, as she moved more of Jess' clothes onto the rack she had put in the corner of the guestroom. *I guess it's having all my chickens in one coop,* she thought with a smile.

Hearing Johnna's vehicle pull into the drive, Lily opened the front door to see her daughter get out of the passenger's side to open the rear door for Calliope. Luke went to Johnna, handed her the bag and car keys, and lifted Calliope from the seat. Lily heard Calliope's protest: "No, let me walk" and Luke's equally firm: "You can walk when we get you in the house—no argument."

Lily rushed to Charlie's play spot on the living room floor and began scooping up toys. "Charlie, pick up your playthings, sweet boy. Mommy and Luke are here with Calliope." They finished just in time for Lily to restrict Charlie to the guestroom doorway, to order Max to "Stay," and to meet the trio in the foyer. Luke set Callie on her feet held but held her elbow to stabilize her, as Lily asked, "Would you like to go lie down, Callie?"

Lily sensed more vacancy in Callie's eyes, as she replied, "Yes, I would."

"Callie, we have prepared a room for you. I hope you will be comfortable while you are staying here." Lily led Callie and Luke to the bedroom, while Johnna and Jess waited with Charlie. "Callie, you have privacy here, a place to study and prepare for your classes, and you and Luke will share the bathroom right outside the door. If you need anything you can't find, just ask me and I'll get it for you."

Lily and Luke watched as Callie shuffled into the bedroom and scanned the environment. "Jeff's drawing," she said, touching the artwork on the wall. Then, she picked up one of the photographs on the dresser and, setting it back in place, she said, "These don't belong here."

"No, Callie," Lily replied, "they don't. But we are having the cabin repaired, and we wanted you to have some of your things while you're staying here."

Calliope went around the bed to the desk, beside which Lily had placed Callie's satchel, and on which lay open the book that had been at her bedside. Callie pushed the switch to turn on the desk lamp, pulled out the chair, and said, "I have some work to do now."

Lily looked to Luke for direction, and he just shrugged and shook his head. "Callie, please, rest soon.

I'll knock on your door when lunch is ready."

Lily watched as Callie open the book while speaking: "I felt upon my feet the chill of acid wind creeping across the sill. So stood longtime, till over me at last came weariness, and all things other passed to make it room."

Lily and Luke left Calliope to reunite with the remnant of her physical collection, knowing there was a multitude of volumes at her disposal in the uniquely rich resource of her mind.

Chapter 54

Jess was excited to have Calliope and Luke living under the same roof with them. She had received her mother's text during lunch break, and she knew "Operation Calliope" was "afoot," as Sherlock would say. Lily would be making Jess' room as conducive to Calliope's needs and comfort as possible, and this evening Jess would move in temporarily with her mom and Charlie. Jess knew her grandmother was changing bedding, hanging Jeff's drawing of the Cultural Arts Center, placing Calliope's photographs on the dresser, and making room in the closet and in a drawer for some of Calliope's clothes. Lily had said Calliope was zealous about cleanliness and almost phobic about germs, and she would wash and wear the same outfit every day, except Calliope knew her colleagues expected her to change daily.

Jess was eager to go home to see Calliope, but as always, she relished her time in Professor Daniels' class. He was adept at putting together geography, history, and the Biblical text into what was, for her, a rich, faith-affirming structure of wisdom and truth that had stood the tests and ravages of eons. Of course, the prescribed studies were not geared toward any specific religion—in the class, she knew there were students of various backgrounds and beliefs, even non-belief. But she could tell from their rapt expressions and thoughtful questions, all the students found the class interesting and enriching. At the end of the period, Jess gathered her materials, secured her backpack, and made her way to the front of the hall to speak to Professor Daniels.

"I guess you heard the news about Calliope?" he stated, seeing her approach. "She should make a full recovery. Good news ... such good news."

"Yes, sir, it is. I'm eager to see her."

"Well, Jess, just a word of advice as Calliope's friend and yours. Don't rush her ... just a calm, measured approach ... maybe ask a question to which she can give a simple, objective answer. She might like to hear about something you've read or studied that would engage her interest and stimulate communication. But she will need and prefer to be alone much of the time. It's good to remember that not only her body must heal, but her mind must overcome the emotional trauma she has experienced. She must process and organize her thoughts and feelings about what happened."

"Yes, sir ... I'll remember," Jess responded.

Noting her puzzled expression, Daniels apologized, "Oh, Jess, I'm sorry. I forgot to flip off my 'Lecture' switch."

"You seem to know a lot about Calliope, Professor Daniels."

"Well, I have done quite a bit of research on personalities like Calliope and have some general understanding. You see, my son, I suspect, is what Calliope was at the age of four, although only in recent years has there been awareness that their characteristics are more than simple 'shyness' or 'social awkwardness' and have behavioral therapies been available. Alex and Calliope, in their individual worlds, always will be unique, gifted, and special to those of us who love them. They have intelligence and talents that may make solid contributions to society. It is our responsibility, as much as possible, to make the world in which they must function, amicable and accommodating of their lifestyles—for them and for the benefit of society."

"That's very interesting, Professor Daniels. I would like to know more about this."

He responded, "Well, you have a full load of schoolwork and little time to spare … but, if you sincerely want to know more, google 'autistic spectrum disorders.' It is a burgeoning field of study and research."

"Thank you, sir. I want to understand Calliope. She is the most interesting person I've ever met, and I would like to learn about 'what makes her tick,' as Grandma would say."

Daniels smiled and locked the flap on his briefcase. "If you, now or in the future, figure out what 'makes them tick,' I want to be among the first to know."

"Yes, sir, count on it," she smiled. As she turned to leave, she asked, "See you soon, Professor?"

"Saturday at the latest," he answered. "Luke and I have an office to plan."

As Jess moved toward the exit, her phone rang and, seeing her mother's name, she answered the call: "Hi, Mom, how's everything going?" Jess listened for some seconds, said, "That's fine. I'll just wait in the Commons. Call me when you get here," and then, asked, "Has she said anything? … Oh, I see … well, maybe her books will help."

Steve Daniels, following behind Jess, asked, "Any news on Calliope?"

"That was Mom telling me she's running late. Calliope's home. She hasn't had much to say—just some strange poem about acid rain creeping through the window."

He seemed startled, when he asked, "You mean 'the chill of acid wind creeping across the sill'?"

"I don't know ... maybe ... something like that."

"Jess, call your mom. Tell her I'm bringing you home and to stay close to Calliope. We'll pick up Alex on the way and be there in about thirty minutes. ... Now, Jess ... call her now."

Jess punched the speed dial on her phone and waited for her mother's voice. She told her mom what Mr. Daniels had said. "She wants to know why, Mr. Daniel."

"Because those are words of Edna St. Vincent Millay ... 'The Suicide.'"

Chapter 55

"Good afternoon, Steve. Come in, come in," Lily urged. Giving Jess a kiss on the cheek, Lily said, "If you have time, Jess, why don't you take the boys and Max out in the yard?"

"Sure, Grandma, just let me put my backpack on the table. I've got some assignments I'll work on later."

Steve asked, "Lily, how is Calliope? Any more communication with her?"

"Johnna's been with her since we got your message. As far as I know, she hasn't said anything more. She's just reading at the desk in the bedroom."

Without further exchange, Steve Daniels went to the bedroom door and knocked. Johnna opened the door, pointed him to the window seat, and left the room, closing the door behind her."

Steve spoke to Calliope's back, when he asked, "What are you reading, Calliope?"

"I don't know," she answered. "I don't see, I feel."

"What do you feel?"

"I don't know. My mind won't still."

Steve said, "Dear Calliope, even now, you are speaking with the soul of a poet. There is not a discordant note in your being."

Calliope turned to look beyond Daniels to the view through the wall of windows behind him. "Lonely I came, and I depart alone, and know not where nor unto whom I go; but that thou canst not follow me I know."

Bounding to his feet, Steve demanded, "Calliope! Stop this!" Looking around, he asked, "Where are your boots?"

"I don't know."

Looking in the closet, Daniels found the battered leather boots, neatly aligned beneath Calliope's meager wardrobe. "Put these on your feet," he ordered.

Calliope stoically obeyed his command.

From the bed, Steve took her denim jacket and hat. "Put these on."

Again, she complied.

"Are you strong enough to go for a walk?"

"Yes."

"We are going to the cabin. But first, look around this room. This is a lovely, light-filled, comfortable room that your family has prepared for you. They love you. They want you to be happy, even if that means letting you be in this room alone. They know it's easier for you to live in your world by yourself than to be with them in theirs. But they are right outside that door if you need them. They will be there when you need them because they love you. Now, come."

Steve led Calliope through the door, calling, "Lily, do you have the keys to Calliope's car and the cabin?"

"Yes, I do," she answered. "Want them?"

"Yes, please."

Lily brought the keys and handed them to Daniels. She was surprised to see Calliope dressed for the outdoors but asked no questions.

"We're just going over the hill to the cabin to get her car and bring it back to your house." He spoke as if their excursion was simply part of a normal day, when there had been no injury, no hospital, and no potential threat to life. Steve took Calliope's arm for support and propulsion toward their destination.

In Calliope's weakened condition, the walk to the cabin was longer than usual. When they arrived, she was breathless and leaned heavily on Steve. "Let's go up the front steps," he said. Unlocking the door, he opened it into the cabin, which looked much the same as the last time Calliope was there, but smoke still permeated the space. "Let's look around, Calliope: The mantel where your photos were … knowing they are important to you, Lily brought them to her house for safekeeping until the cabin is restored. She did that because she loves you. … The walls where Jeff's drawings hung … knowing they are important to you, Lily took all of them to her house, so you could have them near, until you can hang them again here when the cabin is ready for occupancy. … Remember Jeff's drawing that was here next to your office? Lily put it in the room at her house—the room she prepared for you—so you can see it first thing in the morning and last thing at night. Now … here … this is where your office was … Luke and I have plans to put it back just the way it was—the outside construction already has begun. True, it's now just a sad pile of ashes and burned books, but all of which can be replaced—I have your catalogue. More importantly, all that is precious to you is stored right there in that extraordinary mind of yours," he said, tapping her on her forehead. "Your mind and the ability to store it so full of beautiful words and thoughts is God's unique gift to you. You are His 'one of a kind' with your special gifts—and, whether you understand or appreciate the fact, He loves you and your family loves you, because you are Calliope Winchester, the one and only—their 'one and only.'"

Steve waited for a response. Calliope left his side

and went to her former bedroom and opened the closet, now almost empty. Reaching to the top shelf, she felt around on the surface until she found and withdrew a feather. Calliope held it before Steve's face and said, "From uwohali. Let's go now. I need to get my car."

Chapter 56

Their meal would be simple: roast beef sandwiches, chips, and salad, with ice cream, as usual, for dessert. While Steve and Calliope were away, Lily, Johnna, and Jess had met together and determined to conduct themselves in a calm and quiet manner, if Calliope joined them for dinner. Jess had laid the last place setting when Steve knocked, and Calliope came through the door without the formality of greeting. Seeing Jess in the dining area, Calliope strode toward her and held the feather in front of Jess' face. "Recognize this?" she asked.

Jess answered, "Uwohali."

"Right," said Calliope. "You can keep it. ... Lily!" she called, "I'm hungry. I'll go wash my hands."

Wiping her hands on a dish towel, Lily came to the kitchen door and looked at Steve with a puzzled expression: "What in the world ...?"

Steve just responded with a grin and, "What can I say? Maybe 'tough love'?"

After supper, Steve and Alex said their goodbyes—tomorrow would be another school day. Johnna bathed Charlie and tucked him into bed with Max, as usual, by his side. Calliope returned to her room, with the warning that Lily would be checking on her from time to time. Jess laid out her books on the kitchen table, and her mom reminded her, "Jess, be in bed by ten." Fritz lay by Lily in front of the fireplace, as she caught up with the day's news on her tablet. And wrapped in jackets against the evening chill, Luke and Johnna sat side by side in the front porch rockers.

"Do you think we'll be sitting here like this thirty or forty years from now?" Luke asked.

"Well, if we're still here at all," she responded, "we'll likely be sitting somewhere like this, if not here—just rocking and going nowhere fast."

"It's good, though, you know? I can't think of any place I'd rather be. Guess I'm getting old. The Continent, the South Seas, the Far East—the most romantic places on earth, as people say … nope, not any of them has any appeal … just right here … with you."

"Well, Luke Ferguson, there's that romantic streak again—amazing what a starry night and an old rocking chair can do to a man," she laughed.

"You know, that whole get down on one knee thing is for the twenty-somethings, don't you think? How about if I just show you this and ask if you'll accept it?" From his jacket pocket, he took the velvet box and opened it to reveal the ring that had been waiting in his valet. Johnna was so surprised, she could not respond immediately, and he continued in spurts: "I hope it fits. … I had it made just for you. … The blue stone is for Charlie, and the pink one is for Jess—I figure you are a package deal. … You may not be able to give me an answer right now. … You can think about …"

Johnna blurted, "Yes. … Yes, Luke. I will accept it—if that means you come with it," she laughed through her tears, as he slipped the ring on her hand.

"And it fits!" he exclaimed. Luke stood and grabbed Johnna's arms, pulling her to her feet. "Let's be clear: I just proposed, and you said 'Yes.' Is that right?"

"Well, after a fashion. I think the result is the same.

You're going to marry me, Ranger Luke." Johnna gave him a sweet kiss with promise of many more to come. "We need to go tell Jess," Johnna said. "I'll feel completely free and ready to rejoice once she's told and on board."

"Let's go now. I'll follow your lead," he took her hand, kissed it, and led her back into the house." Luke locked the front door behind them and fastened the high latch, allowing Johnna a moment's headway into the kitchen, where Jess was folding her books and packing her backpack.

"Jess, you've got a few minutes before bedtime. Can I talk to you?"

"Sure, Mom. What's up?'

Johnna held out her hand and said, "I just accepted this from Luke. It's an engagement ring. How do you feel about it?"

Jess was stunned. She had thought this day would come, *but—now, right out of the blue? How do I feel? she asked herself. You know ...* she thought ... *I feel happy ... like it's just right and good.* Thinking back to where she had been six months ago, she was surprised that she could do nothing but squeeze her mom and say, "It's great, Mom!" Seeing Luke approaching the kitchen, she ran to give him a bear hug and to say, "I'm really happy—for all of us, Luke."

Lily, who had been watching the scene playing out before her, said, "Well, Johnna, are you going to come over her and let me see that ring on your finger?" Johnna waved her hand before Lily, who whistled and said, "Luke, son—and I do mean 'son'—you've done a fine job of making the deal. Now, you two need to determine the where and when of sealing it. I think Steve Daniels will be your 'go-to' guy for that."

Luke released Johnna's hand and said, "There's

one more person I need to tell." He knocked on Callie's door and heard her respond, "Come in."

Chapter 57

After class, Professor Daniels called Jess to his desk. "I talked to your mother this morning. She and Luke are coming to my house this afternoon to talk about wedding plans. You are to come home with me and meet them there. I just need to pick up Alex on the way."

"What about Calliope?"

"What about Calliope?"

"I guess she's going to use your library while you talk with Mom and Luke?"

"Do you mean to tell me she's here at the college? She's supposed to be recuperating."

"She sure is. She came in with Mom and me this morning. She said she had work to do before her class and I should just meet her in her office after school."

"Well, she never ceases to surprise me. I think I can predict ... anticipate ... a certain behavior from Calliope, and then she stands me on my head!" Picking up his briefcase, he said, "Let's go see how her day went."

"Professor Daniels, have you done many second weddings?" Jess asked as they walked toward the Humanities building. She clarified her question: "Well, for Mom it's a second wedding—a first for Luke. He told Mom he was engaged a long time ago, but it didn't work out."

"Well, I've done quite a few," he answered. "Generally, if a person has had a happy first marriage, the second is happy also, if there is a second. He—or she, has learned how to give and to share—and how to put the partner's needs above his own. Of course, God says, to paraphrase, 'One man and one woman for one lifetime.' Death breaks the marriage bond, as in your mother's situation and in mine."

Pensive, Jess walked along in silence for some moments before asking: "How does my dad figure into all this? Do you think Luke is concerned about how he stacks up against Dad? We've made Dad out to be practically a superhero—that might make Luke feel bad. I hope not—I really love Luke and wouldn't want to hurt him. And do you think Mom feels like she might be betraying Dad? I don't ... not really." She sighed, "I just want them to be happy ... I want us all to be a happy family."

"Well," said Mr. Daniels, "You have been giving this marriage a lot of thought. I think you ought to tell Luke and your mom how you feel—tell Luke you love him and that you are happy—and proud, he is going to be your stepdad. Tell your mom you think your dad would be pleased that a man like Luke is going to be assuming your dad's responsibilities as head of your family."

"I think you're right, Mr. Daniels. I'll do that. ... By the way, what should I call you—'Professor Daniels' or 'Mr. Daniels'?"

"I tell you—call me 'Professor Daniels' when we're at school—teacher and student, and 'Mr. Daniels,' when we're being friends. I am of the older generation who would not think 'Steve' appropriate."

She teased, "I bet you're almost as old as Grandma."

He chuckled, "Yes, and I bet you think she's ancient."

"Oh, you may find this funny: Mom said when Luke told Callie about the marriage, she asked him if

Johnna was going to give him some wool socks."

"Wool socks?" he asked bemused.

"That's what she asked. She said something about Mom's giving him wool socks to prove she'd be a good wife."

Professor Daniels halted his steps to give free rein to his laughter, while Jess waited and wondered what could be so funny. Catching his breath and wiping tears from his eyes, he said, "She likely said, 'Woollen stuffs, by the hand of Evangeline woven. This was the precious dower she would bring to her husband in marriage, better than flocks and herds, being proofs of her skill as a housewife.' Jess, that's from Longfellow's tale 'Evangeline'—you'll study it in literature, perhaps, even memorize some of it. I believe Calliope, in her own inimitable way, was making a scholarly witticism."

"A witticism, huh? Well, too bad it went right over our heads."

Steve welcomed Johnna and Luke into his home with congratulations on their upcoming marriage. Alex came running to the door to collect Charlie, and the boys were gone in a flash of eagerness and enthusiasm to begin their play. "Jess and Calliope are up in the library," Steve informed them. "Jess is taking the opportunity to do some research for a paper I have assigned my class, and Calliope is delving into whatever piques her curiosity. Please, come, have a seat," he said, motioning them to a conversational grouping of loveseat and upholstered armchairs. "Would you like something to drink?" he asked.

"Not for me," replied Luke.

"Nor for me," agreed Johnna. Noticing a photograph of Steve Daniels and his late wife, Angie,

Johnna remarked, "Your wife was a lovely lady. I wish I could have known her. Mother says she just lit up any room with her presence, and she was the first on the doorstep when anyone had a need."

"Yes, she was the dearest on earth to me, and I miss her terribly. I can't imagine trying to deal with such a loss without the strength of faith to know our parting is only for a relatively brief piece of existence." He sighed, "But enough about me. We've got wedding plans to discuss."

Luke spoke up: "We'd like to get married on Thanksgiving morning ... eleven o'clock. That's little more than three weeks away. Would that be a problem for you?"

"No, I don't think so. We don't have any close family to disappoint, and church activities are either before or after Thanksgiving Day."

"That's great," Johnna said. "It will be a simple ceremony, just our immediate family and a couple of friends—on Mom's front porch, weather permitting. Jess will be my maid of honor, and Luke's friend, Jack Collins, the best man. Then, afterward, Mother will host a Thanksgiving buffet reception."

"Oh, that sounds like the makings of a very special occasion." Taking a pad and pen from his coat pocket, Steve said, "Let me just make a few notes ... Thanksgiving Day, 11:00 A. M. ... Oh, better remind myself that's Central Time in your county. ... Okay, as a formality, I have some basic questions I always ask: Luke, this is your first marriage?"

"Yes, I've come close but never crossed the finish line," he quipped.

"And, Johnna, your first marriage ended in the tragic death of your husband, I understand?"

"Yes, that's correct."

216

"I'm so sorry. I empathize with your loss … but I rejoice you have found happiness again."

Johnna took Luke's hand and said, "I have, and I think J. B. would approve my decision, if he could. Luke's a strong, courageous, protective man, who loves me and my children. We will have a strong, happy family, with God's blessing."

"Amen," Steve declared. "Now … will you be writing your own vows?"

"Well, I don't know how Johnna feels about it," Luke promptly responded, "but I'd prefer just to say, 'I will,' 'I do' … whatever … when you ask me."

Johnna laughed: "We'll go with your handling that for us. We'd have to postpone the wedding to give Luke time to write his vows, and then he might not be able to get the words out," she teased. "Besides, he's trying to get the cabin finished before his leave of absence is up."

"Yes, Luke, we've got an office to complete, too. Well, I think we're finished with this," he said, returning his pen and notebook to his pocket. We'll go over any last-minute details at the rehearsal. … There will be a rehearsal?"

"Yes," Johnna replied. "We thought on Tuesday evening … very casual, and Mom will furnish food, as is her 'thing.'"

Johnna and Luke took their cue from Steve and stood, as he was replying, "And she does her 'thing' so very well. I'm still carrying memories of her cooking around my waist. … Before you leave, come see where Calliope and Jess are holed up." They followed Daniels through the kitchen and sunroom to the garage apartment.

Topping the stairs, Johnna said, "Steve, this is beautiful!"

"Thanks. I think sometimes I'm a bit too proud of

my sanctuary and ..." Getting their attention, he nodded toward Calliope. "... the people who visit here. 'For what I figure as success is simple Happiness, The consummate contentment of your mood ...'"

Calliope was leaning back in Steve's desk chair. Without raising her gaze from the volume she held, she continued: "'You may toil with brain and sinew, And though little wealth is win you, If there's health and hope within you—You've made good.'... Robert William Service."

"Hey, Mom, Luke," Jess greeted them. "Isn't this a wonderful place?" Closing her tablet, she said, "I'm just about finished with my paper, Mr. Daniels."

"Good work. You can leave those books on the table, and I'll return them to the shelves later," he said.

"Time to go, Calliope," Luke stated.

"Calliope, take that book with you, if you want. Just make a note of its title on the desk pad."

As the group made their way through the house back to the front door, Steve called to Alex, "It's time for Charlie to go home, son." Soon the boys came running down the hallway to the foyer.

Alex ordered, "Come see my room" and took Calliope's hand. "Come see."

Steve said, "If you all don't mind indulging my son—his room, also, is an interesting space." He smiled, "The operative word is 'space.'"

Alex's room was a large bedroom, enveloped in astronomical posters and paraphernalia. Littering the floor were massive volumes covered by glossy jackets, scattered with sparkling stars or covered with colorful photos of planets. "This is my orrery," he declared with pride, leading them to the model located on the wide shelf of a cubby storage unit. Looking around the floor, he found a folder of clipped and copied pictures; and, taking it to Calliope, he said, "Look. This is a picture of the asteroid, Kalliope. Daddy told me that's your name, too." Calliope took the folder and examined the photo, while Alex continued: "Here is where Charlie and I look at the sky." He pointed to two thick bedrolls lying in the center of the room. "Watch!" he ordered, as he ran to close the door and flipped the light switch, plunging the room into darkness. He plopped himself on a bedroll and pointed to the ceiling: "See!" The constellations appeared above them, sparkling and moving ever so slightly in simulated rotation of the earth. "Calliope, come see."

Calliope came to the place and summarily dropped to the floor next to Alex. Then, Charlie returned to lie next to his friend. Jess ordered, "Make room for one more" and squeezed in next to Calliope.

The adults watched the four with amusement, until Johnna said, "Okay, enough, tomorrow's a school day. We all have to get our rest."

Johnna and Steve laughed when Luke began singing the familiar children's tune, "One of these things is not like the others, One of these things just doesn't belong …"

"I have to correct you, Luke: It should be 'Two of these things are not like the others … Can you guess, children, which two are the aliens?'"

Chapter 58

With Fritz at her side, Lily hiked the path to the cabin, hoping she would find the workers in the final days of restoration. The wedding would be coming up in a week, and she wanted everything finished to the point that, while Luke and Johnna were away on their honeymoon, she could move her things out of the annex and have Calliope resettled and content in her new bedroom and office. Lily had to admit she was excited—not only about Luke and Johnna's having their own home, but about her own new phase of life—the first scene of her final act.

Stationing Fritz on the porch to rest, Lily opened the cabin door on a space now void of cabinets, appliances, furniture, and, thankfully, smoky smell. She noted the floors were clean and restored to their natural beauty. The crew foreman called from the loft, "Hey, Mrs. Craig, we're about ready to get out of your way. Just have to install the kitchen cabinets. The bathroom's done. Want to take look-around to see if it all meets with your approval?"

"Will do, Larry," she replied. "It's looking good from here. I've got appliances coming day after tomorrow and furniture the day after that." She and Larry, the supervisor, had used sheet after sheet of graph paper to lay out a floor plan that would accommodate Lily's kitchen and cabinet space requirements and fit in a table and chairs for eight. Lily had told him, "This may be the last kitchen of my life, but I plan to go out in a blaze of cooking glory!" She had determined not to be extravagant, but to equip the cabin with quality items that would last her for a lifetime and far beyond that for Calliope. She thought, *I couldn't have done this without you, John.* The insurance proceeds alone would have not been enough for all the renovation, but her husband had left her financially secure and free to pursue the things she loved—her benevolent activities, training her beloved dogs, and now, making a new home for her and Calliope.

Lily checked Callie's office area and was pleased to see the roof, the walls, the floor—everything, ready for the custom shelves Steve had designed and built. She would let him know he could start assembling and installing them at his convenience, making sure, if necessary, he could work around the desk and chair that would be on the delivery truck in three days.

Checking out the loft area, Lily was pleased with the tranquil colors of the space. She had directed the workers to sheet-rock the walls and paint them a soft blue, and to install durable beige sisal carpet over the wooden floors. Simple roller blinds matching the walls covered the loft windows. The twin platform bed she had ordered with a memory foam mattress contained storage drawers and, with the nightstand and mirrored dresser, matched the light oak of the closet door. She hoped Callie would find the space relaxing, with nothing to jar or disturb the senses. The beige sheets she had bought were silky soft, the bamboo pillow cooling, and the comforter an ocean-pattern in shades of light blue, beige, and white.

For her own bedroom downstairs, Lily had duplicated the order of Callie's furniture, only in a walnut finish. She would keep the log walls and wood flooring, adding a thick area rug in a floral pattern of beige, burgundy, and teal. She had ordered a white distressed trestle table with a walnut wood top and matching chairs for the eating area and a curved beige sofa and matching armchairs for the living area. Again, she wanted the cabin to be a soothing retreat for Calliope, but Lily would add some colorful rugs and accessories here and there for her own pleasure.

"Larry?" she called.

"In the kitchen, Mrs. Craig."

Lily found him and two workers hanging a white rustic wood corner cabinet in the kitchen. "Oh, I'm going to love those cabinets."

"Hope, so, ma'am," he responded.

She told him, "I've got to get back home and get a few things done before my daughter gets back from picking up my grandson at playschool. But we'll come back later to see the progress. Go ahead and lock up if you leave before we get back."

"Will do, ma'am," he agreed.

Lily stepped out onto the porch and inhaled the fresh autumn air. What a glorious day! she thought. Oh, my, I've got to get back and plan my shopping list—for the rehearsal and for the reception!

"Fritz, come, let's go home," she ordered, as she descended the porch steps. She turned to see he hadn't moved. "Fritz!" She waited, then bounded up the steps to the dog's side. She felt the stillness of his body and saw the vacancy in his sightless eyes. "Fritz! No, no … dear God, please … no!" she cried.

"Mrs. Craig!" Larry called as he opened the door. "Mrs. Craig, what's wrong?" He found Lily kneeling on the porch, rocking back and forth with the upper body of her beloved dog cradled in her arms.

Chapter 59

Johnna met Steve, Jess, and Alex at the door. Giving Jess a kiss on the cheek as she passed, Johnna said, "Hi, Calliope. Alex, Charlie is playing in his bedroom … go on back. Steve, thanks for bringing Jess and Calliope home. Mom had wanted me to see if you could come to dinner this evening and check the progress on the cabin, but now we just need your friendly support—especially mother. She's in the kitchen. I'll go make sure the boys are settled."

Steve, Calliope, and Jess found Lily—her face red and swollen, sitting at the kitchen table. Jess went to wrap her arms around her grandmother and said, "Grandma, I'm so sorry about Fritz."

"Thank you, dear. I knew this could happen. The vet had reminded me Fritz was getting old for his breed—nearly twelve. The snake bite likely weakened his heart. … It was just so unexpected. He seemed to have his strength back … maybe it was just his last burst of life. … I feel like I've lost my best friend."

Steve sat at the table across from Lily and took her hand. "What can I do?"

"Oh, Steve, you've done enough just being here … to help me get my head together. I know Fritz was only an animal, but he was special and an important part of my life for so many years. I know losing a dog is nothing like losing a spouse or a child … or even a human friend—but it still hurts."

Steve agreed, "Of course, it hurts. You know, sad to say, a dog's love and loyalty to his master, his human friend, sometimes can put to shame the love and loyalty of a person's own kin. Our animal friends are part of God's blessings to make this life richer. But, as with all temporal blessings, they must go—their time runs out ... or we move on to timelessness. But we can enjoy them while we are with them and treasure the memories they leave behind."

Calliope moved to stand next to Lily at the table and said: "Farewell to thee! but not farewell, To all my fondest thoughts of thee: Within my heart they still shall dwell; And they shall cheer and comfort me."

Lily remained in Steve's gentle grasp and reached her free hand to take Calliope's. "Dear, you and Steve have such "a way with words," as they say ... perfect words ... comforting ... Thank you."

They heard Luke stomping the dirt from his boots before entering the kitchen door. "It's done, Ms. Lily," he reported. "I put a big rock on the grave up near the mini barn, so you know where to plant flowers when the time's right."

"Thanks, Luke. It's shady enough there, we might even put in another dogwood." Lily took a deep breath. Pressing her weight on the table, she stood and declared: "It's time I get supper going. After we eat, Steve, maybe you and Luke can explain to Charlie what's happened to Fritz." She paused, then observed: "This will be the first experience with death he remembers. He may be concerned about losing Max, too." Lily seemed to shake away troubling thoughts to continue: "After supper, I'm going to recruit the help of my girls." Looking to Callie and Jess, she said, "We're going to put together a shopping list for the rehearsal and reception. ... And, Callie, that includes some new clothes for you!"

After supper, the men gathered in the living area. Steve and Alex sat on the couch. Opposite them in an armchair, Luke sat with Charlie on his lap with Max on the floor next to them. Having cleared the supper dishes, the four women were at the table, listening as Steve and Luke explained to the boys about the meaning of Fritz's life … and death.

Steve lounged on the sofa and casually began: "Alex, do you remember how we talked about your mother's death—about how she got sick and her body died, but she went to live forever in a beautiful, special place?"

Alex replied, "Uh-huh, she can't come back, but we can go see her someday."

"That's right," Steve agreed. "And, Charlie, your first daddy, like Alex's mommy, died too—but just their bodies. People don't go away forever—the 'you' inside your body goes on and on. Your body is just like a little house for the 'you,' the spirit inside your body, until it's time for 'you' to go on to that special place."

Tears began to fill Johnna's eyes when Steve referred to J. B. as Charlie's "first daddy," and she fully appreciated the fact that Luke would be the only father Charlie would know—the man who would be her son's role model through life. As Charlie leaned back against Luke's chest, she knew she had made a right and good decision and that, if it were possible, J. B. would be smiling and nodding in approval.

"Charlie, Max is not like people. God made Max and Fritz and other animals just to live in this world. While we are with them, we can love them and play with them— and they can be our friends and want to be near us. But when their bodies die, they don't have spirits to go live in that special place. We bury their bodies in the ground, and they help make flowers and trees grow for us to enjoy. They don't go on forever, but they give us happiness while they are here and can give us beauty when they die."

"Max is going away?" Charlie asked.

Luke said, "Not any time soon, son, but he will get old and die someday. We will be his friends and be happy with him for as long as he lives."

Steve continued, "Charlie, today Fritz's body died. Luke put his body in the ground, and some beautiful flowers will grow above him."

Charlie whimpered and said, "Fritz is gone?"

"Yes, son, but we will remember our happy times with him. And he has taught Max how to be your friend … how to have happy times and make new memories."

Luke petted Charlie's head when he turned his face to cry on Luke's chest. Johnna knew Charlie would be alright—he might have questions, but she and Luke, together, would be prepared to give him answers.

Johnna looked at those around the table: Jess was sniffling against the upheld hem of her sweater. Lily was dabbing her eyes with the dishtowel she had brought from the kitchen. And Calliope … even Calliope … staring into the space of her personal bubble … the track of a tear glistened on her cheek.

Chapter 60

Lily assessed every detail of the spread before her: She had pushed the table against the wall, freeing chairs to be placed around the living/dining space in comfortable positions for her guests. Backed against the wall on the burgundy cloth, stood a spray of flowers in vibrant autumn colors, around which lay a platter of barbecued pork, bowls of "fixins," pitchers of tea and lemonade, and the "up-scale" paper plates, cups, and napkins on which Johnna had insisted. Lily was not sure she was on-board with this much informality, but she knew it would be easier on her. The reception would be only slightly more involved with the Thanksgiving buffet she planned—but she would make it special, if not elaborate.

"Jess, check the weather report again, please."

Cleaning the kitchen counter, Jess moaned, "Grandma, it hasn't been twenty minutes since we last checked it—high 60's and no rain until Sunday. If the weatherman's right, we'll get through the wedding just fine—don't worry."

"No, no worry ... I pray he's right. ... But we've got to have a backup plan in case he isn't."

Jess huffed as she came from the kitchen to stand in front of the fireplace. "Okay, Grandma ... look: We bring the flowers in from the wedding arch outside and lay them across the mantel. Mr. Daniels stands here. The guests sit on the couch and in the chairs we put behind it. The guitarist and flute player ..."

"Flautist, dear."

"Flute player, flautist … whatever, can set up in the foyer. Luke and Jack Collins can come in from Calliope's room, and the rest of us from the annex."

"Do you think there'll be room for us to get by the guests and to fit up there?" she asked, tracing the path through the space and gesturing toward the fireplace.

"Yes, ma'am. There'll just be Calliope, you, then Charlie, me, and Mom, in that order. Jack Collins will be that way, to Steve's left; I'll be on his right; Charlie will sit with you after he brings in the Bible. So, there only needs to be room for Mr. Daniels with Mom and Luke in front of him."

"Well, you make it all sound simple," Lily sighed.

"Grandma, it is simple." Jess went to her grandmother to give her a hug. "You just need to think about being the gorgeous mother of the gorgeous bride. Have you lined up the ladies to come and handle the reception? You may be planning and preparing the food, but you need to stay out of the kitchen during the wedding."

"I have."

"And does the photographer know when to come—and that he's expected at nine Central Time?"

"Yes, I confirmed with him this morning."

"What else is there to do?"

"Well, tomorrow I'll finish up the food and get instructions ready for my helpers. They're such sweet ladies—widows, like me. They're going to stay after the reception to clean up and then eat leftovers with us. I'll ask Steve and Alex to stay over too."

"That will be nice—kind of an after-wedding party."

"I hope taking this extra day off from school won't

cause you to get behind, dear. I really do appreciate all the help you've been to me today."

"Not at all, Grandma. I've got all weekend to get my work done, and even the TSP teachers seem laid back and ready for a break this week. I've enjoyed helping you … except when you worry and fret," she teased.

* * * * * * *

"Thank you so much. Your music is absolutely exquisite," Lily said, handing the guitarist and flautist a check for their services. "Now, remember, we'd like to start at 10:30 Central Time, Thursday morning." Waving goodbye to them and returning inside, she thought, *Thanksgiving weddings certainly are costly, but I couldn't be more thankful than I will be on Thursday.*

Now, with the rehearsal dinner over and the Collins couple gone, she was ready for more excitement. She hoped everyone was ready for the "unveiling," but she'd have to lay the groundwork first. Johnna, Luke, Jess, and Steve were gathered near the fireplace, as she passed through to knock on Callie's door. "Here we go," Lily said. "Time for some silent prayer," she grinned.

"Callie, may I come in?" she asked.

"Yes, the door is unlocked."

Calliope was sitting at the desk with an open book and notepad. Lily asked, "This has been an interesting day, hasn't it, Callie?"

"They are using my wedding arch. That's good. It's pretty. I knew it would be," she commented.

"Yes, it is. May I sit?" Lily gestured toward the window seat.

"Yes. You want to talk?"

"I do, Callie. I told you your stay here would be temporary, until the cabin was repaired. Well, it is finished. Soon you will be able to go back there."

"Tonight?" she asked.

"No, soon after Johnna and Luke leave on their honeymoon. But there are changes at the cabin, Callie. I hope you understand and will be content with them."

"What changes? I thought it would be like it was before?"

"Callie, let me tell you how it's going to be, then you tell me how you feel about it." Calliope nodded and Lily continued: "I am going to live in the cabin with you, and I have changed it so we may have our own private spaces but help each other, when I need help or when you need help." Callie frowned, so Johnna waited a few seconds and said, "Your office is restored, but I have prepared the upstairs as a special, quiet, relaxing space as a bedroom for you—because I love you and want to please you. I will stay in the bedroom you had before the fire, because stairs may be difficult for me as I get older. We have a lovely new kitchen, where I can fix meals for you when you come home from school, and there is new furniture that is soft and comfortable."

"What about Luke," she asked, "Where will he stay?"

"I am giving this house to Luke and Johnna and the children. They need more space than you and I. While they are away, Steve will help us move your things back to the cabin, and I will move out of the annex and leave it ready for Luke and Johnna when they return." Lily waited.

Calliope stood and moved to the closet to retrieve her boots, jacket, and hat. "Let's go see."

As they passed through the group in front of the fireplace, Lily signaled to them. "Luke, load everyone up. It's showtime!"

Arriving at the cabin, they all assembled on the front porch. Even Charlie and Alex were wriggling with almost Christmas morning excitement. Lily said, "Let me go in first with Calliope, if you don't mind, to show her everything and get an initial reaction ... everything, but the office," she added, nodding with a smile to Steve. "Give us two or three minutes, then come in and look around. We're saving the office for Steve's grand finale." Lily unlocked the door and said, "Charlie, when you come inside, tell Max to stay on the porch."

Lily ushered Calliope into the cabin and waited as Callie walked in front of the fireplace and sat momentarily on the couch. She then went into the kitchen, turned around gazing at the cabinets and appliances, and opened the refrigerator to peer inside. "Where's my bedroom?" she asked.

"In the loft where Luke used to stay," Lily answered, with a silent prayer all would be acceptable and Callie would not be distressed by what she found. "Remember, Callie, I tried to make it something you would like, but if you want to change it, you can." Lily followed Callie up the loft stairs and watched as she ran her hand across the smooth surface of the new dresser. "We'll bring Jeff's drawings back and rehang them ... and your photographs for the mantel." Callie walked to the bed, pressed the mattress, and then plopped down on it. Lily cringed to see the old, battered boots on the clean, new comforter. "Callie, let me show you something. Take off your boots." Callie removed her boots and handed them to Lily. Lily pulled out a storage drawer from the base of the bed. "Look, you have a place you can dedicate to your boots, jacket, and hat."

Callie lay back on the bed and said, "Good, very good. You've done a good job. But I think I need some stars."

"Stars?" Lily was perplexed.

"Stars. Alex has stars. I'm going to get some for my ceiling."

"Ms. Lily, are you two about finished?" Luke called. "We've got another package to unwrap down here."

"We're coming right down," she answered. "Come, Callie, Steve has his very special gift for you."

Steve met Calliope at the bottom of the stairs. "Calliope, you and I still have some work to do, but I believe we've got a good start on your library." He opened her new office door and allowed Calliope to precede him into the renovated room, a smaller version of Steve's own retreat, with white bookcases going to the ceiling. Calliope's eyes seemed to focus on every inch of space, as she made her way around the room, touching the spines of books and the spaces where future volumes would reside. "With your catalogue, I have been able to restore several of your collection—some duplicates from my own or volumes that I don't use much. I thought we'd find it entertaining to search through old bookstores to look for others." When she came to the office ladder, she smiled, and Steve said, "A little something extra—necessary, but also, a special gift for my special friend, Calliope."

Having circuited the room, Calliope sat in the leather desk chair behind an expansive cherry desk. She leaned back in the chair, closed her eyes, and declared: "This is good—very good. Soon, I won't have to borrow your books."

Chapter 61

Thanksgiving morning was the answer to Lily's prayer—clear, crisp, but with the prediction of the sun's warming to high 60's later in the day. Her helpers had arrived on time and had instructions in hand and clearly in mind. They sent Lily out of the kitchen with orders to "Go, get beautified, and leave everything to us." Lily joined Johnna and Jess in the annex, while Luke, Steve, Charlie, and Alex would be joined by Jack Collins when he arrived.

Lily moved around the bedroom straightening, organizing, picking up, folding … "Have you girls got everything you need? Johnna, are your bags in the SUV? Jess, do you need the curling iron? It's in my bathroom. "What about flowers? Oh, no, I forgot the flowers."

Johnna grabbed her mother and set her down in the bedside armchair. "Mother, enough, settle! We have everything we need. The bags are in the SUV. A curling iron is the last thing Jess needs, remember? And flowers? I handled those myself. The guys have their boutonnieres, the bouquets and corsages are there by the dresser, and the florist's assistant should be dressing the arch and setting up chairs in the yard as we speak. After all, I am a grown woman. My mother doesn't have to do everything for me. What is it they say, 'This ain't my first rodeo?' Now, mother, dear, please get yourself dressed. The photographer will be here in twenty minutes. I told him to come in the annex door to take our pre-wedding photos, and he's going to find you a nervous wreck in an ugly old duster, if you don't get ready."

"You think my duster's ugly?" Lily grinned at Jess.

"Well, let's say it ain't nearly as purty as your purple party dress," Johnna quipped. "What about Calliope? Is she going to be ready on time?"

Lily said, "I trust she's getting dressed in her bedroom. She'll join us as soon as she's ready. I'm hoping for the best."

Jess was trying to stay wrinkle-free in her long, teal bridesmaid's dress, in which she felt like Arwen from Lord of the Rings, and Johnna was zipping up her mother's long purple mother of the bride dress, which highlighted her white hair and accentuated her still trim figure. There was a knock on the bedroom door, and Jess opened it to see Calliope in the soft gold gown Lily had bought her for the wedding. Jess had never seen Calliope looking so feminine and beautiful—and, she noted, wearing beige strappy sandals, not beaten-up boots. "I need help with my hair," she stated. Jess had just closed the door when there was another knock and Jess opened it to see Jack Collins wife, Greta. She said to Johnna, "I know you and Luke said, 'No gifts,' but I thought I could at least offer my services—she held up a bag and declared: "Professional Cosmetician and Hair Stylist, Will Travel."

Jess exclaimed, "Oh, wow, that's super!" and Calliope added, "Good, very good."

* * * * * * *

At five minutes before eleven o-clock, the guitarist and flautist ended their pre-wedding program with "Annie's Song" and paused for the few guests to be seated and quiet. Then on the hour, the clear, pure notes of "Pachelbel's Canon in D" sounded; and Steve in his standard, black, "wedding and funeral suit," followed by

Luke and Jack Collins in dark navy suits, exited the front door and took their places on the lower porch, under the arch, now adorned with an overhead swag of autumnal flowers in navy, burgundy, teal, gold, and cream, from which draped sheer cream side panels.

Calliope was the first to come around the corner of the house from the annex. She was a vision in gold, with her long dark braid festooned with extra flowers from the table arrangement. Without regard for keeping pace with the music, she strode up the walk to her assigned place, third seat on the first row to her left. She was followed by Lily, in purple elegance with white hair swept up above dangly earrings. In his "little man's" navy suit, Charlie beamed as he marched toward the archway, presented the Bible to "Alex's daddy," and sat down between Grandma and Calliope.

When Jess appeared, Lily could not restrain the emotion of seeing her granddaughter—so lovely, so grownup ... and remembering ... the tragedy, the disruption of their lives, her granddaughter's nightmares ... her anger and frustration when she tried to bear her burden of grief in solitude. Not even a year had passed, and here they were in a time of joy, celebration, and newness.

Then Steve motioned for the guests to rise, as Johnna appeared to begin her walk to the porch. Lily sobbed when she saw Luke struggling to control his tears. Johnna was resplendent in a long, beige lace trumpet gown with sleeves that flared at the wrist. Her hair was down but lay in soft curls around a matching beige lace hairband with short netting attached. Her bouquet, like the other flowers, was in autumnal shades of blue, burgundy, cream, and purple. Johnna arrived at the altar and gave her hand to Luke. Steve said to the audience, "You may be seated."

The audience listened carefully, captivated by Steve Daniels' dignified, resonant voice and the words he spoke—of strength, encouragement, and commitment, personalized to this couple, their family, and the unique circumstances that had brought them together. From tragedy, they had turned to faith and family. From the disruption and confusion of life, they had sought direction and orderliness in the way of God and His people. Now, they were focused on moving forward, cherishing the best of the past and the promises of the future, but living and relishing every moment in what, they had learned, could be a tenuous present.

As the ceremony concluded, Steve announced: "And now, for the first time, I present Mr. and Mrs. Luke Ferguson." Luke gave Johnna another kiss and began the recessional to the guitarist and flautist's playing "Love and Marriage."

Jess followed her mom and Luke. Then, for the audience's entertainment, Charlie stood and turned toward the audience. Taking a whistle from his pocket, he blew on it, and Max suddenly appeared. To everyone's delight, the dog was wearing a white collar with navy bowtie. He sat at Charlie's signal, and Charlie's little boy voice commanded, "Say 'Thank you,' Max"; and Max barked twice before Charlie said, "Come," and they proceeded out.

Lily's only thought was *Yes! My boys did it!* as she and Calliope finished the recessional and heard Steve announce, "We're all invited for a delicious Thanksgiving buffet, so don't go away."

* * * * * * *

Lily, Steve, Calliope, Jess, and Lily's friends—the kitchen helpers, sat around the dining room table nibbling on leftovers. One of the ladies asked, "How can I keep feeding my face when I am so tired?" and the other responded, "Because you're on your bottom, not your feet, and your hands are free to keep shoveling it in." Even Calliope smiled at their friendly repartee.

Lily said, "Well, Luke and Johnna should be just about at their destination by now."

"Where are they going, Grandma?" Jess asked.

"That's a big secret even I don't know. They just said I have their phone numbers in case of emergency, and they'll check in to make sure all is going well here."

The doorbell rang, and Lily said, "Now, who could that be? I thought we'd be through for the day." She kidded her friends: "We will be as soon as you two hit the road. You know you can take leftovers with you."

Lily answered the door, and a man said, "I have a message for Mrs. Lily Craig."

"Yes, I'm Lily Craig," she replied with a shot of anxiety.

"I'm supposed to read this message to you: 'We thought it only fitting that we should express our deepest thanks to you for all you have done for us, for all you did to make this day perfect, and for the care you will give our children while we are away. This is just a small token of our love, appreciation, and confidence—that what you and Fritz did for Max, you and Max can do for Lucas, whose name means "bringer of light." God bless you. We love you. Luke and Johnna.'"

The man's unseen assistant stepped around the doorway into Lily's sight. He was holding a champion Alsatian puppy with a collar lettered, "Wagner Kennels."

Luke stood with his arm around Johnna as they stood on the Point and looked over the valley below. They had stopped on their way to the Falls to visit the place of their first meeting. "That was a lovely spring day, but this is a perfect autumn day—a day, truly, of Thanksgiving." Johnna teased, "I trust you'll be able to keep my feet warm on those cold winter nights that will be here before long."

"I don't know—that depends on how cold those big feet of yours get on cold winter nights."

"You stinker," she retorted. "I love you—you know that, don't you?"

"Yep, and I love you. I look forward to every moment of the rest of my life with you." With their arms wrapped around each other, they stood for some moments in awe of the beauty of the view before them. "You think Lily has gotten her surprise by now?"

"They should have made the delivery twenty minutes ago. She'll be excited, but Charlie will be hanging from the ceiling!"

"Well, we'd better get on our way. I want to check in before dark."

Johnna turned, then something caught her eye. "Luke, look!"

Swooping and soaring before them, the eagle seemed to be performing solely for their pleasure. "Thank you, sir," Luke said. "You are a handsome, magnificent representative of your species."

Johnna's eyes filled with tears of joy, as she whispered, "Uwohali."

"What?" Luke asked.

"Oh, it's just something Jess told me. It's time to go."

9 781949 472592